CONTENTS

THORN

BEARS OF BURDEN

CANDACE AYERS

LOVESTRUCK ROMANCE

In Burden, Texas, bear shifters Hawthorne, Wyatt, Hutch, Sterling, and Sam are livin' easy.
Beer flows freely; pretty girls are abundant.
The last thing these good ol' bears are thinking about is getting hitched.
Until fate comes knocking...

Allie McMichael is running scared.
Not from monsters in the closet or creepy things under the bed.
She's scared of commitment.

On the run from a would-be fiancé, Allie finds a temp job out in the middle of nowhere.
Love is the furthest thing from her mind until she meets her big, burly boss.

Bear shifter Thorn Canton is a successful tavern owner and confirmed bachelor
To Thorn, a mate might mean a fate worse than death—literally.
But da-yum if that new barmaid isn't wearing down his resolve at every turn.

1

HAWTHORNE

"Check out the blonde in the pink dress." Sterling Mallory whistled under his breath. "Da-yum, she's a looker."

I'd already noticed. I'd also gone back to her place the week before.

I stretched back in my chair and flashed a wide grin. "Go ahead, call her over. It's been what? Twenty minutes since the last time you struck out with a woman? 'Bout time for you to try again."

Sterling's big brother, Hutch, clapped me on the back and huffed a laugh. "Twenty minutes? Hell, you must've missed that bouncy little redhead not ten minutes ago."

Sterling shook his head. "She was a lesbian. Don't count as striking out."

It counted. I slid a glance towards the bar. Abram, my assistant manager, nodded. Everything was fine, which meant I could stay and relax for a bit longer in my favorite chair at the corner table with my lifelong buddies, Sterling, Hutch, Sam and...

"Where's Wyatt?"

Sterling ignored me and left his chair to approach the blonde, who was eyeing me, a coy smile playing at the corners of her lips. I just shook my head and tipped my old John Deere cap at her. Sure, she was a beauty, but I wasn't about to give false impressions. I didn't go back for seconds.

"Last I knew, Wyatt was headed up the mountain with another group of would-be survivalists."

A shudder ran down my back. "How he deals with some of those crazies, I'll never know. I swear that bear attracts the nut-jobs."

Hutch nodded and then nearly snorted out his beer. The pretty blonde had just slapped the hell out of Sterling. "Another strike out. Looks like little brother is going home alone tonight."

"Nah. He always manages to find himself a pity screw." Even as the words left my mouth, a tall brunette came up to Sterling and cupped his bright red cheek. "See. I don't get it, but some women love the wounded ego thing."

The ear-splitting sound of shattering glass echoed through the place followed by a collective groan from a group sitting at one of the tables up near the juke box. As the crowd parted, I spotted Cammie rushing to clean up a massive mess of spilled beer and broken mugs. From what it looked like, she'd dropped an entire tray of drinks. *Damn.*

Sam Jennings chose that moment to plop down in his usual seat beside me. He followed my eyes to Cammie and her disaster and shook his head. "What's that? The fourth time this week?"

I pushed off from my chair and stretched out my legs. "Fifth. I don't think this is going to work out."

I left them sitting there and joined Abram at the bar. He'd been my assistant manager for years and knew what I wanted before I did most of the time. "What's the deal with her?"

His eyes went to Cammie then trailed over to Sam. "Your buddy bedded her and hasn't called her back."

Fuck. I had a strict policy about my friends staying the hell away from my waitresses. It was hard enough to keep good help around, what with dealing with a bar full of drunk shifters, and humans alike, day after day. I glared over at my best friend and decided I was going to bleed him later.

"Think she'll bounce back?"

Abram expertly shuffled a few beers into customers' waiting hands. "Not a chance. She's already told me tonight's her last night."

I grunted. At least she was going to finish her shift. That was more than they normally did.

As if she'd heard my thoughts, Cammie plunked the tray she'd been carrying onto the bar and without a word, without even meeting my eyes, yanked the apron off her hips, and tossed it on top of the tray before turning and sprinting out the front door.

"Dammit."

Abram laughed like it was the funniest thing he'd ever seen. He slid another couple of beers down the bar and shook his head. "Looks like you just got a promotion, Boss. I don't reckon that apron is going to fit you, though."

I tossed the apron towards the bin of soiled towels and picked up the tray. "Do we have some resumes left over from last time we hired?"

"I'll figure it out," he nodded, "You just get your cute little butt out there and earn you some tips!"

I flipped him off and grabbed several beers, assuming that's what most of my patrons would be drinking. When I stopped by my table, Sam looked up at me with a hangdog grin.

"Sorry, Thorn. I didn't expect her to run."

I smacked him on the back of the head and handed a beer to Hutch. "Keep your fucking dick away from my waitresses, Sam. This shit is getting old. I got a business to run."

He still didn't manage to wipe the grin off his face. She must've been worth my ire. I shook my head and headed back to the bar, ready for what would no doubt be a long night.

The little blonde cut me off and smiled up at me. "Hey, Thorn."

The pink dress she had on certainly did hike up her girls, and I found them distracting as hell. "Hey."

"I haven't heard from you so I thought I'd stop back by and say hello. I had a lot of fun the other night."

I let a crooked smile tilt my mouth. "Me too."

She rested her hand on my arm and batted her eyelashes. "I'm free later tonight."

Damn. I looked around the bar and saw how busy it was. By the time the night ended I'd be exhausted and cranky. I decided that it'd be kinda nice to have a little something soft and warm waiting on me. I slipped my arm around her side, brushed my lips against her ear, and growled, "I'll come around to your house after I close up."

She shivered and pressed herself against me. "I'll be here. Just find me when you're finished."

I watched her saunter over to her friends before I turned back to the bar. Abram had been observing with a grin on his face. When I got back to the bar, he just laughed.

"You're just as bad as Sam. Only difference is you don't screw the waitresses."

Which was the point.

2

ALLIE

Texas. Hmm... not exactly where I'd planned on ending up, but, then, I didn't really have a plan to speak of. Who knows, this might just be the hand of fate guiding me, right here. *Burden*, Texas. Hell, the name alone seemed to foreshadow my destiny.

I'd run out of gas on the side of the road with absolutely no money left in my bank account. My sporadic road trip was just that - completely and utterly sporadic. I'd thrown a few things in the back of my old Mustang and just headed the old girl west. What I hadn't done was make sure I had the finances for my travels.

My phone died somewhere in the middle of Arkansas and I'd left the charger back in North Carolina. The snacks I'd packed had been depleted in Tennessee. I'd grown tired of sleeping in my car the first half of Texas.

I'd gotten off the interstate in Arkansas to enjoy the scenery and crossed over to Texas in the same way, on back roads. Going through the small towns had been stunning, until I found myself on the side of the road, stranded with not another soul in sight.

I'd just passed the sign for Burden when the damn car sputtered to a stop. I looked around and rolled my shoulders. The outskirts of

Big Bend National Park had spectacular views. Burden was at the bottom of the far west side of Texas, on the Mexican border. I'd driven far off the beaten path for a chance to see Big Bend and now, here I was, stranded in what was potentially a ghost town.

I wasn't entirely sure it was abandoned, since I didn't actually know the first thing about Burden, Texas. I think I remembered seeing it on the road atlas I'd studied at a gas station outside of Austin. But, I'd driven through several ghost towns that had also been listed on the atlas, so the prospects of Burden actually being inhabited was somewhere around fifty-fifty.

Anxiety started to wear at the edges of my consciousness. I snatched my backpack from the trunk and tossed it over my shoulder. I'd hike through the park and hope to find a park ranger. Hiking the last thirty miles into Big Bend hadn't been my plan, but then again, I didn't exactly have a plan. And besides, this trip just might be my very last taste of freedom. The last chance I had to throw caution to the wind. My final hurrah as it were.

It was May, so not the hottest month of the year, but the daytime temperature was still in the high nineties. I'd dressed in simple, loose cotton shorts that morning that stopped just below my ass and a spaghetti strapped tank top. My clothes were perfect for the weather. My flip flops sucked for hiking. No matter, I tied my hair out of my face with a bandana and marched on.

This might be an unexpected hiccup, but I wasn't one to let something like this get me down. Sure, it sucked to break down. Even more so outside a place called Burden, a place that was probably just some rugged land with a few abandoned adobe style structures on it. But, technically I was still on the road, which had been the point of leaving in the first place. To experience an adventure. I wanted to see everything. I wanted to spend as long as I could seeing everything.

It had nothing to do with me running scared from the marriage proposal my boyfriend had sprung on me. Nope. Nothing at all.

Summer hadn't taken over yet and wildflowers were still blooming on each side of the road. As I walked, the blooms charmed me and I couldn't help but smile. Green grass blew in the hot breeze.

In the distance, the road dipped and I lost sight of whatever it was that I was walking towards. Only when I got closer, could I see the town spread out in the valley below.

Burden looked like a perfect little town. I could see enough movement to convince me that it wasn't an abandoned ghost town. Awesome luck!

With a pep in my step, and my flip-flops slapping the soles of my feet, I headed towards this little slice of salvation. The first structure I came across was a large log cabin style place. A rustic wooden sign mounted over the door read 'The Cave'. I peeked in the window, and the sight of neon beer signs made me feel like I'd won the lottery. Looks like I wasn't gonna die from heat stroke or dehydration out in the middle of Nowhere, Texas after all.

A few cars dotted the side lot, enough to indicate that the establishment was open. I stepped up onto the wide porch that wrapped around both sides of the cabin, and as I did, I felt an air of familiarity swirl around me and waft its way over my senses. An intimacy settled over me and I stood still for a second to try to make sense of it. I'd never been to Texas before, what was it about The Cave that felt so incredibly like déjà vu?

Worn planks of wood stretched out under my feet and creaked when I shifted my weight back and forth. I caught the slight whine of an old country song, along with the aroma of pine and grilled steak which elicited a loud growl from my stomach. I had no business feeling homesick for a place like this one, but there it was. I was feeling homesick for a place I'd never been.

It had to be a mind trick. That was it. My mind was finding comfort anywhere that wasn't back home. Anywhere that wasn't filled with chaotic, plaguing thoughts and fears. Yep. This was simply a town that didn't threaten my piece of mind, a town where I could pretend that I had no problems or worries. Except an empty bank account and an empty gas tank.

I shrugged my backpack higher on my shoulder and pushed through the front door. The Cave was surprisingly dark for midday. Natural lighting from the windows lit the front of the place, casting long streaks of light across wooden tables and chairs and leaving the untouched areas in shadow. Old chandeliers hung from the ceiling, unlit, and a large jukebox took up part of the corner opposite the bar.

Several pairs of eyes looked up when I came in, but almost immediately lost interest in me. Except one pair. The bartender stared at me and used his knuckle to lift his hat a bit. His lips curled in a friendly smile after a few seconds so I made my way over to him.

"New in town?" He was older, probably in his mid-fifties, and had a surprisingly gentle voice. I kinda liked him already. He looked the part of a rough and tumble bartender in a Texas border town, but his demeanor instantly put me at ease.

"Yeah. I was driving through to Big Bend and ran out of gas. Luckily, this place was close."

He narrowed his eyes and looked at me thoughtfully. "Most people don't drive this way 'round for Big Bend. Hell, most people don't have the time to. You always pick the longest way 'round to somethin'?"

I laughed through my nose, thinking not just of my entire trip, but my entire life. "I guess so."

"So, you just needin' some gas?"

A lanky kid in a chef's coat shuffled past carrying a giant steak. I tried hard not to stare. I put a hand to my stomach to muffle the grumblings and had to focus my eyes on the surface of the bar top to get my thoughts together again.

"Actually, I need some kind of temp job. Do you know anywhere around here that could use some help?"

"Thought you was just driving through?"

I shrugged. "I was. Until I ran out of gas... and out of *money* for gas."

He gave me a questioning look. "Not many folks get in their car and travel the long way around places without knowing they got enough gas to get where they're going."

"Yeah. Umm... I didn't really have a destination in mind when I got in the car. It was just one of those last-minute things."

He shifted his weight, leaned against the bar, and studied me through narrowed eyes.

"You got a boyfriend chasing you down?"

My stomach clenched. "Doubt it."

"The law after you?"

I grinned then and shook my head. "Not even a little bit."

"You on any kind of drugs that make you crazy enough to get in your car and drive without gas money to get where you're goin'?"

"Nope. It's all natural."

"Then you're hired. Had a waitress quit on me last night and I could use the help."

The feeling of familiarity crept back over me, and something else, belonging.

"You're serious?"

He nodded and held his hand out to me. "I'm Abram. Assistant manager. You ever waitressed or bartended before?"

"Yes sir, a time or two," I slid my hand into his, "Allie."

3

ALLIE

Abram made a big deal out of feeding me before I began working. I wanted to be all reticent and act like I wasn't starving half to death, but I couldn't do it and voraciously scarfed down the burger and fries he brought out to me. After I downed a tall glass of ice water, I came around to his side of the bar.

I'd worked in bars since I was sixteen. I was one of those girls who'd developed early and looked older than she was, so I got away with it in the dive bars on the outskirts of Charlotte. I made quick work of my first task which was mentally cataloguing where everything was located, then set out to make sure Abram would not be sorry he'd offered me the job.

I was overwhelmed with the unusual feeling of belonging. I didn't know what it meant, but I wasn't going to argue with fate, and right then and there, I felt like I'd been guided by the unseen hand of destiny to The Cave, deep in southwest Texas. For how long, who knew?

"We're mostly a 'shot and a beer' establishment, but we do get our cocktail people. You know any recipes?"

I grinned. "Try me."

He slid a glass down to me and nodded to it. "Long Island."

It took me a bit longer than it normally would, since I was still getting used to the bar, but I had the drink back in his hand in less than a minute and a half.

He took a long swig and nodded. "I think you'll do."

Abram had kind eyes and he seemed to take an instant liking to me. We talked about the tables, the food, and how he'd pay me. The atmosphere was easy and laid back. Abram made a specific point of warning me about 'fraternizing', as he put it, with the owner's friends.

"Avoid those idiots. Thorn has a strict rule about employees dating his buddies. They're not exactly the love them and keep them type, if you know what I mean. Sons-of-bitches cost me the last three waitresses."

I looked toward the table where he was pointing and rolled my eyes. "Not interested, I can assure you," I muttered. I had enough going on, as it was. The last thing I need was more complications.

Abram raised his arms to the air and mouthed a 'thank you' to the ceiling. "Any plans on where you'll be staying?"

I shrugged. "I've been sleeping in my car, so I figured I'd keep doing that. I just need to find a place to shower and I'll be good. I don't require much."

He looked thoughtful but didn't say anything. Instead, he nodded towards a big, burly guy who'd just entered. "Here you go. Your first customer."

I turned an easy smile on the man arriving at the bar. "Hey, there. What can I get you?"

His eyes slid to Abram and then to me again. "Well, well, what do we have here?"

"Name's Allie. Now, what'll it be?"

The man's face suddenly split into a wide grin. "I think you got a feisty one, Abe."

I read the man as a beer guy so I reached under the counter and grabbed a bottle. "Domestic?"

His eyes lit up and he took the bottle from me. "She even guessed my beer. I think this one's a keeper."

"Would you like anything to eat?"

He leaned forward. "Can you guess that, too, little lady?"

I rolled my eyes and slipped the order pad from my apron. "I'm all out of guesses. What'll you have?"

Another couple of minutes passed with him teasing me instead of giving me his order. As soon as another patron entered, I tore the top sheet off my pad and slapped it onto the bar in front of the burly guy who'd introduced himself as Big Bob. "Well, Bob, when you figure out what you want, you write it down. Don't seem like you're in any hurry, so I'll just grab it on the way back around."

I heard Abram snort and Big Bob grunt. Big Bob seemed harmless, like he just wanted to play and flirt a bit, but I'd been working in bars for a little over ten years. I'd learned which men to shut down and which ones to let carry on. Big Bob had to be shut down or he'd take it as far as he could.

I got the new customer's order and carried it back to the kitchen. The chef, Brady, nodded to me to let me know he got it. When I got back to the bar, Big Bob had scribbled across the order sheet. I rewrote his chicken scratch underneath, clearer, and smiled my friendliest waitress grin at him.

"Thank you. I'll get it out to you soon."

The afternoon continued on like that. I learned the who's who of the regulars, which patrons to keep an eye on, and oriented myself with the bar. In short, the afternoon flew by and before I knew it, it was already dinnertime. People filled the bar for their meals and then stayed to drink.

"Is it always this busy on a random Thursday night?"

Abram looked up from pouring a drink. "Yup. Pretty much. This is the only place in town that serves food. It's the only bar, too, so every day is busy."

"Wow. The owner is a genius. When will I meet him?"

"Thorn? He should be in any time. He had a long night." There was something in the way Abram said it that made me think it wasn't only work that'd occupied the boss's long night.

I ran another round of food to a table and collected a few tabs at the bar before returning to the conversation with Abram. "So, the owner, Thorn, he's a lot like his buddies, then?"

Abram seemed surprised and then thoughtful. His eyes crinkled at the corners as he snickered. "I guess so. You're fast on your toes, aren't you? You sure you'll want to move on eventually? I could use someone like you around here on a permanent basis."

I shrugged. "I'll stick around for a few days and then see."

"Me and the wife have a travel trailer that we use once a year to go up to Colorado. Keep it over at a spot not too far from here." He looked up from pouring a beer and met my eyes. "You're welcome to use it. There are hookups there for water and everything."

I stopped what I was doing and turned to face him full on. "You're serious?"

He nodded. "No one should be sleeping in their car out here. The weather is crazy. Wouldn't want my best new employee freezing to death or getting washed away by a flash flood."

I threw my arms around him in a tight hug and then slunk back to where I'd been, like it never happened. "Thank you, Abram. I really appreciate it."

"Don't thank me yet. You'll have to stay until closing with me so I can take you over to it and help get y'all set up."

"That's perfect, Abram. Turns out my schedule is completely clear. The only thing on the agenda for today is work."

He patted my shoulder as he moved past. "Work the bar for a while, would you? Boss just got in. I've got to bend his ear real quick."

I waved him away and grabbed a clean rag to wipe down the bar while I had a lag in orders. I had a sudden attack of nervous flutters filling my stomach for some unknown reason. Maybe it was because I was about to meet my new boss. Odd, I wasn't the nervous type. That must be it, though, a little insecurity that perhaps my boss wouldn't be pleased with Abram's choice.

No worries, I'd win him over if I had to.

4

HAWTHORNE

I had the mother's mother of all headaches. Half was a hangover from drinking the night before and half was from a morning of pure hell. There was a reason I didn't sleep with the same woman more than once. Yet, I'd broken my own rule with the little blonde last night, simply because she was there and she was easy, and I'd paid a high price for it. When will I learn? Easy is *never* easy.

I woke up to her cooking breakfast in my kitchen. My completely barren kitchen. I still didn't know where she'd found the shit to cook for us. When I told her I had errands to run, she was annoyed and said she thought we were going to spend the day together. I had no clue where she got that idea from, but I, polite as can be, told her that I was busy and that we most certainly were *not* spending the day together. That got me a plate of eggs flung at my head. She'd seemed so sweet while we were throwing back shots of whiskey.

After she hollered all sorts of obscenities at me for a while, she insisted on using my shower and then taking off with one of my favorite shirts. Annoyance bubbled up in me at the recent memory, but I kept it in check. It was my own fault.

Instead of my usual morning run through the woods and breakfast at Wyatt's mom's place, I'd spent the morning cleaning up over-easy eggs and trying to get a psycho chick out of my house. Which was another mistake. I never brought women back to my place.

So far, the day had been a total train wreck.

There'd also been a nagging tingling at the back of my neck all day. I figured it was bear not getting a chance to get out and run, but I wasn't sure. Something had me on edge, that much *was* for sure. What I needed was to shift and roam the woods, maybe find a berry bush to sit beside and snack off of.

Duty called, though. I had to meet and greet the new girl Abram had texted me about. I parked around the back of the bar and entered that way. Brady was at the chef station, his gloved hands working on battering a couple of pieces of fish.

"All good back here?"

Brady grinned and nodded. "Going smooth, Boss. The new girl is fucking awesome."

I took a deep breath in, trying to sniff her out. What I scented had me grabbing the counter next to me. My dick was instantly rock hard, trying to bust free of my jeans.

What. The. Hell?

I isolated out the scents of everyone I knew. It wasn't hard in a town the size of Burden. My nose locked in on hers almost instantly. She smelled like flowers and something wilder. Freer. Something that reminded me of shifting at the top of a mountain, experiencing a tidal wave of fresh, sweet freedom.

"You okay, Boss?"

I cleared my throat and kept my body arched in so he wouldn't see the tent in my pants. "Sure."

Abram came through the doorway just then. "About time you dragged yourself in here. You okay?"

I grunted. Okay was relative. "Fine."

He gave me a look, but didn't push. "Allie's the best waitress *and* bartender we've found in a while. I like her. So, keep your buddies away from her."

I hadn't even met the woman yet, and the idea of my friends

hitting on her sent shards of irritation coursing through me. "They won't bother her."

He paused and frowned. "That applies to you, too."

I snarled at him, my frustration and long morning getting the best of me. "Abram!"

He held up his hands and backed away. "Alright."

Abram went back into the bar while I tried to get a hold of myself. I needed to eat something and get some water in my system. That would help. "Will you send a plate out for me, Brady?"

Brady acted like he hadn't just heard me being an asshole. "Sure thing, Boss. I'll send it out with Allie."

I felt, more than heard, the rest of the gang come in and settle at our table. Abram's comment stuck in my craw and I intended to make sure they left my new waitress alone.

I forced myself to head straight to our table. Something I couldn't explain fizzled underneath my skin, working my jangled nerves to the max. I wasn't sure what it was. Shifters didn't usually get sick; whatever we might pick up was quickly killed off by our incredible healing abilities, but maybe I'd caught something exceptionally nasty. Something my immune system was struggling with. The guys were already seated at our table, all eyes focused behind me. Annoyance gnawed at me because I knew who they were watching.

"Keep your eyes to yourselves, assholes. You know the rules. Even if some of you insist on breaking them." I dropped into my usual chair, still refusing to look up at the new waitress.

Hutch slapped my shoulder. "Can't blame a man for looking, right?"

I could hear the appreciation in his voice and blew out a rough breath. "Already order?"

They laughed, but Sam grunted. "Abram ran over here like a bat out of hell. Refused to let her anywhere near us. Like we're some kind of sex-crazed beasts."

Wyatt was sitting across from me, freshly returned from his survival weekend tour. "Well..."

I laughed and shook my head. "I'm due for a major run tonight. Anybody else?"

Sterling swore under his breath. "Oh, shit. That slap-happy blonde from yesterday is here and she looks pissed. You think she's still mad at me? Jesus, some women can hold a grudge."

My eyes lifted just as she stopped at our table, another pink dress hugging her curves. Her hair was pulled back in a style that intentionally spotlighted a hickey I was pretty sure I hadn't left on her the night before. I leaned back in my chair, arms across my chest, and crossed my legs at the ankle.

"Thorn."

I opened my mouth to say her name and realized that I had no clue what it was. "Hey...you."

Hutch snorted and leaned into the table. "This just gets better and better."

"Are you kidding me? You don't even remember my name?!" Her voice got louder and a whole hell of a lot shriller.

My shifter hearing was sensitive and this chick was about to burst my eardrums. "Can we please talk without all the hollerin'?"

My request just seemed to wind her up more. She'd drawn all eyes to herself with her first bout of yelling and was obviously enjoying the attention. Just as she was about to open her mouth for a second round, though, a body slid between the blonde and myself.

"Well, hey there. I've got a bottle of Jack behind the counter with your name on it. Why don't you c'mon over there and let me pour you a glass?"

God, her voice. It was breathy and a little husky in a way that had me wondering what it sounded like right after a full night of fucking. It sent chills through me and invigorated the hard on I'd only just gotten rid of.

I couldn't see her face, but what I could see was definitely working. Her full, round ass was enough to have my mouth watering. I had the instant urge to bite it and take her from behind while digging my fingers into her soft, sweet flesh. I wondered if she'd be into spanking. *Damn, was I drooling?*

Before I knew what was happening, she was escorting the blonde away. I wanted to protest and beg her to come back and sit down on my lap. Jesus, I'd lost all decorum and sense of morals. All I could focus my thoughts on was what she might taste like if I were to eat her out from behind. What the hell was with that woman's scent that invaded my senses and demolished every last bit of my rational thought?

If I didn't get my shit together, I'd be staring down the barrel of a sexual harassment suit. If Abram didn't kill me first.

5

ALLIE

"He took me back to his place this time and I thought that meant he and I were getting a little more serious, you know? Then, he kicked me out and wasn't even sorry about it. So, I went and slept with my ex."

I handed a beer to another customer and took his money. "Change?"

He shook his head no while making a pained face towards the pretty blonde in front of me. I winked at him and turned my attention back to her.

"Well, was it good?"

She made a confused face. "Huh?"

I leaned my elbows on the bar and grinned at her. "Your sex-with-the-ex, was it good?"

She tilted her head to display a giant hickey. "I mean, yeah. We were together for a while, so he knows what I like. It wasn't as good as it was with Thorn, though."

I held my finger to her lips and shook my head. "We're not talking about Thorn. We're talking about the ex. The beefcake who gave you a great big orgasm today, right?"

She slowly smiled. "I guess so."

"So, it sounds to me like you had great sex today. And now I'm buying you a shot. Looks like you're having a pretty good day."

She tossed out a little chortle and nodded. "Well, when you look at it like that."

"I do. And you should, too. Now, down that shot, girl."

She threw it back and giggled. "It's just too bad my ex has a girl-friend now."

I sighed. "Alrighty, you clearly need more than that one shot. You need an intervention."

A couple stepped up to the bar a few feet down and waved a twenty in the air. I patted Blondie's hand and went to take their order. After I served them and took my payment, I went back to find her on her phone. It was open to a text and she was typing fast and furiously, as though her life depended on it.

"What are you doing now?"

"Umm," she looked up and shrugged, "Not texting my ex."

"Coming from someone who's ridden the ex-train all the way to 'Beating a Dead Horse' Station and beyond, don't do it. Get while the goin's good. Take the great sex you had today and run."

"What am I supposed to do all alone?"

I gestured to the dance floor that was slowly filling up. "Honey, look around. This town's overrun with hot men. Pick one. Preferably a single one. Then just have some fun."

She motioned for me to pour her another shot and then stood up to take it. "You're right. I'm going to go find me a hot single man."

I shook my head as she turned around and then rolled my eyes. Blondie was attractive and meant well, but the girl was a hot mess. And I definitely knew how to recognize one of those. Lord knows, I'd walked by enough mirrors in my time.

I completely understood why she'd lost her damn marbles over the man she called Thorn. My boss, it seemed. With looks like his, the man could certainly set a girl's panties aflame. *My* panties, to be specific. The moment he'd walked past the bar, my eyes were magnets, stuck to his chiseled steel physique.

He was a tall, broad glass of water and my body was behaving as though it'd been stranded in the desert for years. Well, most of me. There was one part that most certainly had not remained dry.

Without the distraction of Blondie, I couldn't help but take a sneak-peek back at boss man. His head was covered by a John Deere baseball cap, and he wore it low on his forehead so I couldn't make out his eyes, but his mouth... Oh, my, I could write poetry about that man's lips. Full and soft looking, set in the middle of a dark scruff of facial hair, the plump buggers were begging to be kissed.

He sported an outdoor tan and I imagined smelling the sun on his skin. When I'd stood in front of him, I almost thought I *had* smelled sunshine.

One of his buddies looked up at me and I quickly lowered my gaze, determined to not appear as though I was checking him out. Because if there was one thing I recognized in the man they called Thorn, it was that he was a player. Player had been my type for so long that I could practically sniff one out from a mile away. It was just the way the world turned. If I was attracted to a man, he was a player. And I was definitely attracted to Thorn.

I shook off the heady lust I was drowning in, and ignored the heat of a set of eyes on my back so I could focus on my job. *Yes, Allie, you have a job to do, and ogling the boss isn't going to keep you employed.*

Brady called an order up through the window to the kitchen and I slipped away from the bar to retrieve it. Abram was stationed at the other side, chatting with an older gentleman and I didn't want to bother him.

"Hey, this is for Thorn. You know which one he is?"

I barely resisted snorting. "I think I can find him."

Brady shot me a knowing look and nodded. "Sure, you can."

I shook my head and sauntered off towards the one table I seriously wanted to avoid. Even just anticipating getting close to the man had my skin prickling with goosebumps and the hair at the back of my neck standing on end. Not to mention my nipples hardening almost painfully and my heart racing. All responses I'd rather do without when having to face a man like Thorn.

I wasn't a girl who usually backed down from challenges, though. Unless that challenge was marrying her on again, off again boyfriend.

I walked right up to him and bent over slightly to put his plate in front of him. "I guess I should introduce myself, boss. I'm Allie."

He tipped his head back to look up at me, exposing two of the brightest green eyes I'd ever seen. Thick lashes surrounded them, thick enough to make most women sick with envy. They narrowed on me and I felt a flush run through me as all the blood in my body heated to a temperature that felt way past boiling. My lungs and heart were squeezing together to make room for the raw lust that instantly arose from the depths of my being.

I didn't need to breath, right? It would seem that I'd crossed over into a place where my lungs felt no pressure at all to get air into them.

"Hawthorne."

His deep voice raked its nails down my back eliciting the sweetest chill. It shocked me out of my stupor.

I suddenly realized I'd been bent over in front of him for... who knows how long, just staring into his bright green eyes. With a gasp of air, I stood up straight and hurried to the other side of the table. I rested my hand on the shoulder of the guy in front of me, desperately needing something solid to bring me back down to Earth. I thought I heard a low growl, like from a wild animal, but that just played witness to how much I'd lost it.

"Do ya'll need anything else?" I forced my eyes to move to each man at the table, except Thorn. "A more permanent bodyguard, maybe? Just in case there are more angry Barbie's lurking."

6

HAWTHORNE

I f she didn't stop touching Sterling, I was going to rip his fucking shoulder off. He was casting a cocky ass smirk at me like he'd won some kind of game. This was no game, though. She was hands off for him. Fuck. She was hands off for me, too. I didn't know how the hell that was going to work out. Not with the insane chemistry between us. I knew I wasn't the only one feeling it. I'd smelled her sweet arousal and it'd been heaven to my nose. The thought that she'd become aroused for *me* made my dick feel like it was going to explode. I shifted in my seat and tried to get her to meet my eyes again.

"That was smooth of you. Do you always run interference with your boss's jilted women?" Sam was looking up at her with way too much interest on his face. They all had too much interest on their faces. Fuckers.

"Only the lucky ones. The rest I leave to the sharp, manicured nails of karma."

Yeah, that had bite to it. I cocked my head to the side and just watched her. No makeup and in a simple bandana, she was beautiful. Her hair was a few shades lighter than mine and wisps managed to fly freely around her face, despite the bandana. Her hazel eyes bounced around the table, never landing on me. Her eyebrows were full and curved and they gave her a constantly challenging look, especially with the way she kept her full lips pressed together, like she was thinking of ways to verbally eviscerate anyone who crossed her. I couldn't keep from picturing myself spanking her again.

I'd missed what Sterling said, but it'd made her laugh. The shit-stain. I balled my hands into fists and stared at Allie, daring her to look at me again. I needed to see if sparks flew every time our eyes met.

It was like she knew what I was up to, though. She refused to look at me, so I pushed it. "Where are you from, Allie?"

She stared at a spot on my shoulder. "North Carolina."

Sam suddenly grinned up at her. "I spent a summer there when I was young. It's pretty."

She nodded. "Sure."

"What brought you here?"

Again, she looked at my shoulder. "I'm driving across the country."

Wyatt perked up. "Alone?"

"Yep. Just me and my lonesome. I ran out of gas this morning just on the outskirts of town. Abram was nice enough to hire me on the spot so I could earn some money."

"Where are you staying?" My question silenced the table and she finally met my eyes again. Oh, fuck, sparks my ass, burning flames of raw desire were incinerating me.

"Abram got me all set up." She bit her lower lip and then released it and looked away from me. She had to feel it too, didn't she? "Well, I'm going to get back to work. Wouldn't want my boss thinking I'm not earning my wages. Ya'll need anything else before I leave?"

Fuck, yes. I needed everyone in the bar to get the hell out so I could breathe again without worrying about someone touching her.

Sterling nodded. "Just a promise that you'll come back."

Allie's eye roll was almost comical. She patted the top of his head like he was a dog and then turned and went back behind the bar. I kept my eyes on her until she was back at Abram's side. Abram was mated. She was safe with him.

"I think it's safe to say *someone* has a crush."

I looked over at Sam and shook my head. "Nah, she's probably just nervous because I'm her boss."

He snorted. "I meant you, jackass."

The rest of the guys laughed and I had to crack a smile. I *was* being a jackass. I felt more drunk with her standing in front of me than I had last night after half a fifth of whiskey. "Shit."

Wyatt gave me a weird look. "You good, man?"

I didn't know if good was the word. "I'm going to run to the back for a second. I'll be back."

They grabbed at my food as soon as I stood up, but I wasn't hungry for food. Not anymore. On the way, I slapped Sterling on the back of the head for flirting with Allie.

I slipped into the kitchen, threw open the fridge door and stuck my head inside for a few seconds. "Jesus."

"You okay, boss?"

No. My skin was on fire. My bear was practically running a damn marathon inside of me. What the fuck was going on? I knew skipping my run this morning had been a mistake. "Sure."

I headed to my office and slammed the door. I needed distance from that woman. I needed space and a few minutes to get myself together. I hadn't felt so out of control of my bear since I'd gone through puberty.

My office was a sanctuary. Locked behind the thick wooden door, I could almost pretend that I didn't smell her. Sitting in my chair, I looked around and felt a restlessness unlike any I'd ever felt. I was so on edge that I was worried about having a stroke or something. I had recently turned thirty-eight. Maybe I was experiencing some kind of curse. Lord knew my father hadn't lived to forty.

I stretched out as best as I could in the small room and then stood up. Nothing was helping. Maybe I was sick. Maybe it was a fever that had my skin feeling two sizes too small. I knew there was Tylenol behind the counter. I'd take a few of them, see if they had any effect with my shifter metabolism.

I strolled through the kitchen and jerked open the door to the bar just as Allie was trying to push it open. She stumbled, fell into my chest and gasped.

I understood completely. Feeling her chest crush against mine had me wanting to gasp, too. I could feel her nipples pebble against me and it sent white hot lust pulsing through my already feverish body. I caught her easily and took advantage of the chance to wrap my arms around her soft curves. Amazingly, the erratic, restless feeling in my chest faded slightly.

Allie's wide eyes looked up at me and her lips parted. "Oh."

Something primal and unrestrained pumped through my blood. My bear growled. I watched as the sound drew goosebumps to her skin and the aroma of her arousal once again flooded my senses. Her fingers dug into my chest and her tongue stroked out to wet her lips. It took everything in me not to follow the trail her tongue made with my own.

Her body felt phenomenal pressed up against mine and I was too weak to stop my hands from trailing farther down, until the tips of my fingers were on the top of her ass.

Allie's pupils dilated and I knew she was right there with me, feeling the same wild hunger as I was. Just as I was about to throw out the no sleeping with waitresses or bartenders rule, her sweet little mouth opened again and uttered a string of words that not only shrunk my dick, but had my bear tearing apart my insides.

"I have a fiancé."

7

ALLIE

T horn growled again, low in his throat, just loud enough for me to hear it. I should've been freaked out, but instead, I wanted to climb him like a stripper pole. Everything about the man was intoxicating. And off limits. Off limits. Totally and completely off limits. Which was why I'd blurted out the thing about having a fiancé.

Remembering that little tidbit caused my cheeks to heat up but my brain was able to kick into gear again. I let go of his shirt and pushed away from him. "Sorry I bumped into you."

Like that was all that'd happened. Like I would ever *not* feel his fingertips on my ass, or his massive erection pressed against my stomach, thick and heavy and ready to go.

I squeezed around him and tried to act normal as I walked up to Brady, who'd clearly been watching us, and grabbed a tray of food. "Thanks. Table three?"

Brady nodded and kept right on staring.

I turned to head back out, but Thorn was still standing frozen to the spot where he'd been before, as if I'd never moved. I edged around him and sucked in as best I could to avoid touching him again. There was something about him that made the slightest physical contact drive me crazy enough to imagine all the ways we could smoosh our bodies together.

"Allie."

I shivered when he said my name. "Boss?"

"You're done for the night. You can go."

I spun around to face him. "What? I can't. Abram is taking me to his trailer to get it set up tonight."

"He can go, too."

His eyes were an even brighter green than they'd been at the table and his body was nearly vibrating. He wouldn't meet my gaze anymore, either.

I wanted to demand a reason for his behavior, but he was my boss. I couldn't exactly demand anything, especially not on my first day. Not if I wanted to keep my job. Instead, I shoved the tray into his chest and tossed my apron on the counter beside him. "Table three," I said. "I'll tell Abram we've been dismissed."

Of course, Abram didn't believe me. He stuck around to see what the deal was with Thorn, but Thorn just yelled at him and then stormed across the bar to a tall brunette who wasted no time in attempting to suck his face off.

Bitter fury flooded my body, but I tamped it down. I had no right to feel angry or jealous. I had been telling the truth about having a fiancé. Sort of. Thorn could do whatever he wanted. Thorn was not my business.

Even as I formulated my conviction, the brunette came up for air looking like the luckiest woman on earth. She threw her arms around Thorn's neck and pulled him back in for another go. It wasn't hard to imagine them ending up in the back of his truck before the night ended. Or, maybe against the walk-in in the back. *Stop, Allie, just stop.*

I jerked away from the display and headed outside to wait for Abram. The night air had gone frigid and I immediately dug around in my backpack for a sweater. The only one I could find was stretched and ripped all to hell and back so it fell off my shoulder and left almost as much skin exposed as if I hadn't put it on at all.

"Jesus, he's in real fine form tonight." Abram looked at me and shook his head. "You got any idea why I was just kicked out of the bar? That place is going to be a damn wreck in the morning. And guess who isn't going to be there to clean it up. Mr. Hawthorne Canton. He'll be at home, sleeping off another damn bender."

I winced and followed behind Abram. "We had a run in in the kitchen, but it shouldn't have caused that reaction."

"What kind of run in?"

"I bumped into him. That was pretty much it. I mentioned I'm engaged."

He cocked his head at me. "Well, congrats. Even though I'm not sure I should be congratulating you. I don't reckon many newly engaged women go running off for a spur of the moment cross country drive by themselves."

I blew out a big breath. "I haven't accepted yet."

Abram made an unpleasant tsk sound with his tongue. "Damn, woman. You've got a cruel streak in you. What'd that boy at home do to make you run off and leave him hanging like that?"

I climbed into his truck and reached for the seatbelt, only to find it missing. I motioned towards it when he got in, but he just shook his head. "Okay... Um... Well, he didn't *do* anything, I guess. I don't know. He's a lawyer. From a wealthy family. Already owns his own home and it's huge. On paper, I guess he's great."

Abram started the truck and it shimmied to life. "You don't seem too enthused, though."

Eric was probably sprawled in his king-size bed back home in North Carolina tucked under the Egyptian cotton sheets that his housecleaner, Kelly, laundered every other day. Or, maybe he was still up pouring over a case and glancing occasionally at the clock on the bedside table, wondering why I hadn't called to check in.

He was probably in his college T-shirt and the flannel pajama bottoms I'd given him for Christmas three years ago, and there was probably an empty whiskey glass caught, forgotten, between his legs.

"I don't know... there's a lot of history there."

Picking up that I wanted to drop it, Abram just adjusted the static-filled radio station to one slightly less broken up. "I still don't understand why Thorn went all jackass. He should be thrilled that you're engaged and not going to be tempted by his friends. One less chance of you being run off."

I didn't say anything and Abram cleared his throat. "Unless, of course, *he's* interested in you."

I kept my eyes straight forward and sighed. "I don't know about that, either."

He laughed. "Convenient."

8

ALLIE

Abram gave me a tour of the little trailer and worked to get everything set up for me. By the time he left, I had running water, heat, and electricity, and was cozy and comfortable snuggled in the camper-bed that was like a giant pillow.

I slept better than I had in weeks.

I woke up the next morning and showered in the tiny, but clean, shower. Afterwards, I dressed in ripped up jeans and threw my old sweater over my head. It was warming up quickly outside, but the air still held a chill and I figured I'd hike up to my car a bit later to get more clothes.

I didn't have a clue what time it was, but I headed towards the bar, anyway. It wasn't a very long walk, at all, and it gave me the opportunity to look around Burden a little bit. The town seemed to be mostly still asleep. Everything was quiet, until I got closer to the bar.

I froze as Thorn jogged out of the woods beside the bar without a shirt on. His body was drenched in sweat, despite the cool weather. In just loose jersey shorts and tennis shoes, his hair was a little longer than I expected it to be and damp tendrils hung over his eyes.

He stopped and ran his hand through it, pushing it back. Then he turned to face me and another low growl reached my ears. His eyes narrowed on me and his presence seemed to grow even larger.

My eyes were drawn shamelessly to his glistening six pack abs and the deep V of muscle that led right down beneath the waistline of his low-slung shorts. I tried to remember to breath normally and swore under my breath. The man was too tempting.

He stepped closer to me and I got a whiff of his scent, male sweat and something darker. "You look like you were attacked."

I glanced down at my clothes and forced a casual shrug. In reality, I was just realizing how much bare skin the rips exposed.

"You're up early."

I nodded. "I had a lot of free time last night. My boss let me go early."

Another step closer and I could see individual droplets of sweat rolling down his abs. "Sounds like a great guy."

"Something like that." I looked away and blew out a rough breath. "I'd better go. I'm going to help Abram get set up this morning."

"Abram won't be in until around nine. You're a couple of hours early."

"Damn." I crossed my arms over my chest and sighed. "I guess I'll go to my car and get more of my stuff while I'm waiting."

Thorn watched as I walked past him and then he fell into step beside me. "I just finished my run. I'll go with you."

My body reacted, of course. A warm tingling began to spread from the flutter in my chest, down my belly and shot like a missile to the nerve endings right between my legs. I ignored the wetness pooling between my thighs. It had no business being there. "I'm really okay, Thorn. It's just right up the hill."

He shrugged. "Then it's not far for me, is it? Come on."

I had to take two steps for every one of his and I found myself panting by the time we got to the top of the hill. "Slow down, would you? I'm not exactly in the best shape."

He swung around and his eyes raked over me, undressing me in one sweep. When he met my gaze again, his pupils were dilated. "There's not a thing wrong with your shape."

My face heated and I turned back to the road. "Keep your eyes to yourself, would you?"

A low chuckle came from behind me as he followed, slower than before. "Why? Because you're engaged?"

There was that word. I looked down at my bare finger and then back at my car, parked just up ahead. "Yep. Here it is. I just need to get a few items out of the back."

Thorn stood beside me and watched as I jimmied the trunk open and started grabbing clothes. Things were just tossed in, chaotically. A bra here, jeans there.

"You left in a big hurry, huh?"

I made my way around to the front and grabbed a Ralph Lauren shopping bag from the back seat. I tossed the sweater I was supposed to return for Eric onto the floorboard and went back to the trunk so I could gather more stuff. "Yeah. I've been wanting to travel the country for a while. An opportunity arose and I took it."

Thorn reached into the trunk and pulled out a tiny pink nightie. He held it up on the tip of his finger and raised an eyebrow. "An opportunity that had you pack a nightie, but not enough gas money for the whole trip?"

I snatched it from him and threw it into the deepest part of the trunk. "It was a last-minute opportunity."

"I'd say." He took the bag from me and held it open while I shoved more stuff into it. "Where is this fiancé of yours?"

I grabbed more things that I thought I might need and then slammed the trunk closed. "Home, in North Carolina."

He grunted. "If I had a woman like you, I can promise you that I wouldn't be sitting at home if you were on the road, halfway across the country."

I snorted to hide the way his words affected me. "Bullshit. I saw you last night. You had one woman ready to claw your face off when you walked in and another ready to take off her clothes for you by the time I left. You'd never have a woman like me because I prefer more of a commitment from my men. You know, like breakfast and maybe dinner the next day?"

"More of a commitment, as in a ring that you don't wear and a home that you leave in what appears to be the fastest escape in the record books?"

I spun on him and jabbed him in the chest with a finger. "Don't act like you know my relationship. You have no clue why I'm not wearing my ring, or why I left."

"So, you *did* leave?"

"What? Not like that! I just... I just wanted to see the country. My fiancé is a very busy man, unable to just drop everything for a cross-country road trip adventure."

Thorn dropped my bag and stepped closer, crowding me against the side of my car and using his body to box me in. "Why aren't you wearing a ring?"

He was so close I could feel his breath and my mind went blank. He pressed in closer until his thighs were brushing mine and his arms stroked my shoulders as he closed them in on either side of me. I made the mistake of looking up, into his eyes, and felt myself get lost. Thoughts escaped me and I suddenly felt like I was floating.

He slowly lowered his mouth, closing the distance between us. When he was just centimeters from my lips, he flicked his gaze between them and my eyes. His eyes were shockingly green from that close, and burned with intensity. I had the feeling that I'd been trapped, cornered like prey, but damned if I didn't like it. My body was practically humming against his.

"You'll have to forgive me later. I just can't help myself." Thorn ran a finger under my jaw and then used it to angle my face towards his. Slowly, giving me every chance to stop him, he closed the gap between us and roughly tugged my bottom lip between his, sucking and licking before pressing his lips to mine more firmly. *Oh, sweet Jesus.*

His few days' worth of beard tickled my face, but his soft lips were pure seduction. He moved them sensually against mine, pressing firmly into me before licking the seam of my lips. I opened for him and he swept into my mouth with ease, his tongue stroking mine in a way I felt straight down to my core.

I coiled tightly around his body, somehow finding my arms and legs clinging to him. My heart beat a wild, uneven tune in my chest. I'd never felt anything like the power that was surging through us. The way my body was tingling, it was like I could spontaneously orgasm. Spontaneous orgasm. Was that even a thing?

Thorn's fingers raked through my hair and he gripped it tightly, tugging my head back as his searing lips kissed their way down my throat, roughly. His teeth scraped my skin and I cried out in a voice I didn't recognize. The urge to have him sink his teeth into me rolled over me like a tidal wave and I arched my back pushing my throat further into his mouth.

9

HAWTHORNE

My teeth elongated, my bear clawed its way forward, and I opened my mouth wider to sink my canines into the tantalizing woman in my arms. She set my soul on fire. Molten hot lava coursed through my body and the only way to ease the burn was to sink my teeth into her soft flesh. I wanted to mark her and make her forget anyone else.

My bear growled and I let it out before lowering my mouth to her shoulder. Just a little more pressure and she would be claimed. My dick pulsed painfully and I gripped her hair harder, feeling my control slip.

Just as the tips of my sharp canines pierced her tender flesh drawing droplets of blood, a car sped past and blared its horn at us. I froze, but it roused Allie from her lust induced haze.

She jerked away from me and ripped her hair from my hands in an attempt to fully untangle our bodies. With a yelp of pain, she freed herself and snatched up her shopping bag as she stomped away from me looking horrified and confused. I could hear her heart, its unsteady beat calling to me. The scent of her arousal, the flaming pink tinge of her cheeks, the thin trickles of blood dripping from the tiny punctures, a few strands of her hair still intertwined through my fingers, everything about her called to me. To my bear.

He demanded I chase her down and finish what I'd started. Claim her, give her my permanent mark, pin her to a tree trunk and mate her. Fucking bear had no finesse and damned if I wasn't right there with him.

I stared after her, frozen to my spot, and gaped as I finally heard what my bear had been shouting, but I had been too fucking stubborn to hear. Mine.

Mine.

There was no ignoring the shouting in my head now. Allie was my mate. My fucking mate. The realization was a punch to the gut.

Allie continued to stomp off, no hesitating or looking back at me. She was probably thinking about her fiancé. Her fiancé...

I slipped into the woods, desperate to shift and run off the searing pain that was scorching my body. I couldn't stop the wild roar that escaped my twisting, contorting face.

It wasn't until I had shifted and was standing as bear, looking after my mate, that I realized with horror my mistake. I'd allowed my bear to take control of my body. I now had no chance of keeping him away from Allie.

I ran in the direction of her overpoweringly heady scent which managed to pull every primal urge I possessed to the surface. I was seconds from breaking through the trees when I was slammed, caught sideways by the full force of a raging bear and sent sprawling into a massive tree trunk.

The tree rocked and shook from the blow, but I quickly righted myself and with a loud roar, charged toward the offending bear. My protective instincts were on high alert, and this bear was too close to my mate. That wouldn't do.

Instead of fighting back, the other bear shifted to a human and I was left staring down at Wyatt. I snarled at him before forcing my bear to recede. "What the fuck, Wyatt?"

He sat up and glared at me. "What the fuck, *Hawthorne?!* You were charging at your new waitress! What were you planning to do?"

I knew that I didn't want to confide the truth to Wyatt. The truth that my new waitress was also my mate. I couldn't identify why I felt the need for secrecy. Normally, I was an open book. I told my best friends everything. Hell, we'd grown up together and had been through thick and thin. We pretty much knew everything about each other. None of them had mates, though. None of them wanted a mate, as far as I knew. I didn't want a mate.

My bear growled at me and paced back and forth inside, pissed that I wasn't going after Allie. I stared at the spot she'd disappeared from and shoved my hands through my hair. I liked my life. I did what I wanted, when I wanted. I could always find a warm and willing female for me to sleep next to, if I wanted, but on nights I wanted to be alone, I got to sleep alone. I was free. Uncomplicated. A mate would bring more stress, tension, and responsibility than I knew what to do with. Not to mention, possibly cost me more than I could afford to lose.

Plus, Allie was just passing through *and* she had a fiancé.

"Well?"

"I wasn't running after her. I was just running. I didn't see her until it was too late." We both knew he could hear the lie in my voice.

Wyatt shoved me and walked away from me. "You've never lied to me before, Thorn. Get your shit together."

I puffed out my chest and flipped him the bird. "My shit is together. Perfectly together."

"Whatever. Just don't forget about the game tonight."

Fuck. I forgot.

I STAYED the hell away from the bar, despite my restless, pain in the ass bear demanding I go and find my mate. My bear could shovel shit. I wasn't cut out to be mated. I couldn't deny how good Allie felt against me, but she was engaged to some other asshole. I refused to follow my momma's footsteps and latch on to someone who might completely negate my entire existence just by saying goodbye. Besides, I was having the time of my life not being tied down. Fun times, no strings, no one to tear my heart out and send me to an early grave from devastating loss.

Nope. Nothing about Allie and I sounded like a good match.

I just had to avoid her. It wouldn't be that hard. I'd make sure Abram put her on the daytime shifts and I'd come in late. No big deal.

Except, apparently, my bear wasn't on board with that plan. I found myself turning in the direction of the bar. If I breathed in too deeply, I could still smell her. This whole thing was torture.

Until Wyatt's reminder, I'd almost forgotten about the hometown football game. A lot of the shifters in town liked to get together and knock each other around as hard as we could one night a week. The guys and I were on an undefeated team so far. It was always a good time and I even shut the bar down for a couple of hours and sold beer from a big cooler on the sidelines.

The local high school wasn't large enough for its own football field, so we used the field behind the bar. The location made it easy to get supplies from the bar out to the crowd.

Football night was cherished. Shifters naturally had a little extra violence in them, so being able to take it out on one another on the field was always fun. It could get messy and a little bloody, but it was all just for the fun of the game.

After the tension I had built up inside from fighting with my bear to stay away from Allie all day, I needed a release. That was why, fifteen minutes before the games were supposed to start, I was already on the field in just my shorts and tennis shoes, ready to go.

Wyatt was next to me, giving me weird side-glances, but none of the other guys noticed or cared. We were all energetic before a game. Most of the time we ended up matched against a couple of guys we'd never gotten along with and it was a hell of a lot of fun to take them down.

I thought I was feeling better and looking forward to some ass kicking, but then Allie walked out of the back door of the bar, her round ass calling to me as she bent over, wrestling the cooler out. She was wearing a short skirt that kept catching in the breeze. The way it flirted around the bottom of her ass cheeks had me damn near choking on my own spit.

Of course, Sterling and Sam made no qualms about taking in the sight. Just as a bigger breeze blew, her skirt floated up for a second, giving us all a view of her perfect ass, beautifully wrapped in a pair of lacey panties. My dick tented my thin shorts and I couldn't contain the growl that emanated from my chest and rumbled across the field.

As if on cue, Allie stood up straight and ran her hands down the back of her skirt, smoothing it, before turning and meeting my eyes. Her face flushed pink and she spun back around to the cooler.

"What I wouldn't do to take a bite out of that sweet, sweet ass."

I turned and punched Sam in the arm as hard I could. He winced and shoved me.

"What the hell, man?"

"Don't talk about my-" What could I say? "Waitress like that." Instead of arguing it anymore, and playing chance with losing my cool any more than I already had, I hurried over to Allie to help.

10

ALLIE

N o, no, no. I didn't want Thorn's help. I heard him do that growly thingy he seemed to do as normally as breathing and couldn't help the wild crazy stirring of my body responding to it. What the hell was wrong with me?

I kept my head down and tried to remain calm. As calm as I could be when my mind knew just how it felt to have Thorn's tongue explore my mouth.

"Here. Let me give you a hand with that." His deep voice washed over me like a caress and I ended up dropping the cooler and backing away, afraid of how my body would react if he happened to touch me. "Thanks."

He bent over to grab the handle and looked up from his near eye-level position with me. His pupils dilated and he made a sound, from the back of his throat, that resembled a choking gasp. "Your, uh... Your skirt keeps flying up."

I used both hands to hold down the bottom of my skirt, frustrated that I'd chosen to wear it for a night outside. Heat blossomed across my chest and I swore. "Yep. That's happening."

He looked around us, at all the people gathered, all the shirtless men milling about. "Hold on a second."

I watched his muscled, tattooed back disappear into the bar and swallowed hard. He was stunning. If there'd ever been a man who could literally incinerate my panties, it was Thorn. And I hated it. He was so obviously a player. *Of course*, I was attracted to him.

I groaned and looked up at the darkening sky. There hadn't been a cloud around all day long. It'd warmed up since my walk that morning, but it was getting cooler again with the sun fading.

"Here. You can tie this around. It should help."

I took the large flannel shirt from Thorn's outstretched hand and tied it around my waist, eager to keep from showing my ass to all of Burden. I flashed him a small smile and looked away. "Thanks. I'll get it back to you tonight."

"What? You can't look at me now?" He easily lifted the cooler and walked it towards the makeshift bar at the side of the field.

I blew out a rough breath. "Of course, I can look at you."

"Then do it."

I forced myself to look over at him, but seeing his arms stretched taut with the cooler, his muscles flexing, did things to me. I clenched my thighs together and stumbled. More heat took over my neck and face and I was sure everyone around could tell I was blushing and stumbling around like some teenage idiot.

"Smooth." He put the cooler down and then moved closer to me. His breath washed over my neck and chest as he sighed. "Should I apologize for this morning?"

I made the mistake of looking up at him and met his bright eyes. Those eyes. Instantly entranced, I shifted my body to face his full on and chewed on my bottom lip. "Sure."

He moved impossibly closer, somehow still not touching me. "Did you enjoy it?"

Of course, I'd enjoyed it. I'd enjoyed it so much that I'd had to go back to the trailer and change panties. I'd never been so stimulated by a kiss in my life. I'd enjoyed it so much that I almost didn't feel guilty when I thought of Eric, sitting at his desk in his corner office, growing more and more agitated that I wasn't calling. I'd enjoyed it so much that when Kayla, another waitress, offered to let me use her charger to recharge my phone, I'd refused.

I jumped when Thorn's big hand landed on my hip. Even through the fabric of my shirt, it felt like fire. I blinked a few times and tried to remember why I was saying no to him. "I have a fiancé."

Something darkened in his eyes and he backed away. "So you said."

I watched him jog back to the other side of the field and then shook myself out of it. No matter what, I wasn't hooking up with Thorn. Sleeping with the boss was a one-way street to getting fired and being back in my car. I wasn't ready to end my trip. I should've known better than to let another man kiss me while I was sort of engaged to Eric. I wasn't behaving any better than the men who'd hurt me.

I didn't know how to forget the way he'd made me feel that morning, though. It hadn't felt like a simple kiss. It had felt like Thorn was capturing a part of me, or something equally inappropriate. To feel that kind of attachment after one kiss was insane. Impossible. Yet...I'd spent my entire day thinking about Thorn, feeling the same familiarity and belonging to him that I felt to his bar. It was driving me nuts. There shouldn't have been anything. He was an attractive man, sure, but I wasn't a boy-crazy school girl having a first crush. Admiring his sexy physique was one thing, but the wild lust that I felt when I looked at him? Certifiably nuts!

Abram showed up while I was lost in thought and gave me a hand setting up the table for the night. The game started shortly after, two teams of guys I didn't recognize tearing up the field. I watched while passing out beers and taking money.

The game was intense. The men didn't hold back their aggression. They took the opposing teams down with enough force to seriously injure. Yet, time and time again, the players kept getting up and going again. I didn't know how they were doing it.

"It's not as tough as it looks."

I turned to find a man I didn't recognize staring down at me with interest. Something about the way he held himself put me on alert, too much confidence oozing out of his pores like oil of narcissism.

His eyes travelled my body, leaving an almost palpable trail of ick behind. "Taking hits like that isn't hard. Especially not when you're taking them from pussies like Thorn and his pals."

I looked over to where the guys were lining up, getting ready to head out onto the field themselves. "You think *those* men are pussies?"

The slimy stranger combed his hair back with his fingers in a way that I could tell was practiced and nodded. "Yeah, I do."

I took in his sleeveless shirt, jersey shorts, and tennis shoes. He wasn't dressed much differently than the guys playing, he didn't look different, but there was something about him that bothered me and made him stink with ugly. "Do you need a beer or..."

He grinned. "That the only way I'm going to get you to talk to me? Buy one of Hawthorn's cheap beers?"

I raised my eyebrows and put my hands on my hips. "You've got a problem with the beer?"

"Here. Take this and keep the change. You go ahead and have the beer yourself, if you're thirsty. My treat." He handed me a twenty and then, when I didn't take it, shoved it into the pocket on the front of my apron. "Let's talk about something other than those idiots. When did you get into town?"

I was going to lose my shit on him. As stressed as I already was with my lust for Thorn growing by the minute, I couldn't handle some jerk being all weird with me. "You want a beer, I'll sell you a beer. You want to talk, go find a therapist. I'm working here. And, take your twenty back. I'm not accepting tips tonight."

11

HAWTHORNE

"Fucking Kyle Barns is talking to your new girl." Wyatt shook his head and popped his knuckles. "It looks like she's giving him a hard time, though."

I didn't need his commentary. I'd seen Kyle approach her and was struggling with the urge to run over and bash his face into the table in between them. I'd crushed a football with one hand when I saw him slip the tips of his fingers into her apron. I knew she could take care of herself, but I was feeling like I was about to go ballistic, I wanted to go to her so bad.

I watched as they talked more and then Allie tossed the money he'd slipped into her apron at his face. It bounced off Kyle's nose and landed between them on the table. Kyle's back grew stiff as he leaned down with his palms on the table and spoke to her.

Before I even knew what I was doing, I was crossing the field, interrupting the game in progress, and reaching for him. Turned out Allie didn't need me, though. As I watched, she grabbed the neck of a bottle, smashed the bottom of it against the table and then held the makeshift weapon between their bodies.

"Threaten me again and I'll cut your dick off. And if I don't, Thorn will. Isn't that right, Thorn?" Her voice was strong and full of the fire that reflected in her eyes. Her hand didn't shake as it held the broken bottle, sharp end pointed at Kyle.

"Gladly." My voice was a low growl. "Get going, Kyle. I'd hate to cause a scene."

He stayed where he was, facing Allie and I could feel it getting to her. "Run along, little bear. I've got business to finish with the lady."

He shifted his fingers on the table and it was all I needed. I grabbed him by the back of his neck and threw him away from her. A shriek escaped her soft mouth and I vowed to make it right before the day ended. That mouth was made for sounds of pleasure, not fear.

Kyle spun around to face me, but I was already planting the bottom of my shoe on his chest. He went flying backwards and I followed, muscles expanding and threatening to shift. "Stand down, Kyle. Unless you want to thoroughly embarrass yourself."

He climbed to his feet and I let him. "Afraid of a little competition, Thorn?"

Competition? For Allie. He'd die painfully before I let him lay a finger on her. My bear would never allow it. "If you know what's good for you, you'll turn tail and head home."

He leered, practically bearing his teeth at me. "You think you're the shit, don't you? I should show you just how untrue that is."

I was just about to show him just how far he was pushing me, but Sterling and Sam appeared at my side with Wyatt and Hutch behind them. Hutch stepped behind me and squeezed my shoulders. "Relax, brother. This punk is leaving."

Wyatt crossed his arms. "Right?"

And just that quickly, it ended. Kyle was a fool and was going to need to be reminded of just how far down the rankings he really was, but he wasn't crazy enough to try to take on all of us. Most likely, he wasn't even crazy enough to try to take on just me alone. So, when he turned to leave, we let him go.

"I'm getting really fucking tired of his shit."

I looked at Sterling and rolled my eyes. "You did that."

Sterling started rambling about how it wasn't his fault, but we all knew the truth. Sterling poked his pecker in the wrong place and that place happened to be Kyle's girlfriend. Since then, the man had had it out for us. He'd made it his mission to fuck with us every chance he got.

"Well, either way, looks like their team is one down to play us."

I glanced back at Allie and then to Hutch. "Nope, we're down one, too. I'm going to take Allie inside and make sure she's okay. Play this first game without me."

They tried to hassle me about it, but I ignored them. Even though I knew what I needed to do, I couldn't do it. I couldn't stay away from her. That little cry of hers was echoing around my head like a fucking bullet to the brain.

She was still standing where she'd been, the bottle at her side. I finally noticed the way her fingers were now trembling and eased the bottle from her.

"Come inside with me for a second. We'll make sure you're okay." I tossed the bottle away and took her small hand in mine. Warmth spread from my stomach out and I had to swallow back a groan. She was going to be the death of me. I couldn't have her, but my body didn't understand that. My bear sure as hell didn't.

She let me lead her inside the back door and into the bar. I figured she could use a shot after all that excitement. "Where'd you learn that nifty little bottle trick?"

A shaky laugh escaped her mouth. "What? That's not normal? Your daddy didn't get into bar brawls in front of you when you were young?

I looked over at my shoulder at her while grabbing a bottle of whiskey. "My old man was more of the leaving type. Though, I'm sure he did participate in many a bar fight. Just not around here."

She was quiet until I slid a shot in front of her. "What's this?"

I picked it up and held it to her mouth. "Your hands. You're trembling. Figured you could use something to knock the edge off."

Amazingly, she parted her lips and let me tip the liquid into her waiting mouth. Her throat worked as she swallowed it down, drawing my eyes to it. "That guy was such a dick. What was his problem?"

I threw back a shot of my own and pushed the bottle away. It wasn't enough. Nothing was enough to dull the aching desire I felt for her. It pulsed through me until it felt like this physical entity wrapping around my throat, leaving me no chance of getting away unscathed.

"Thorn?"

I shook my head to clear it. "He's just an asshole. What did he say to you?"

"He just told me I was nothing and that he could have me in a second if he really wanted me. Something like no one would stop him because he's the best, yada, yada, yada."

I ground my teeth together and clenched my fists. "I'm going to kill him."

Allie shook her head and then looked up at me. A sudden wide grin spread across her face. "You should've seen his face when I broke that bottle."

Anger left my body in an instant, replaced with scorching heat. Her beautiful smile nearly brought me to my knees. I was an idiot for thinking I could be near her and not touch her. "Allie..."

Her eyes widened but she didn't leave. It was the sign I needed. Or didn't need. I didn't know what I was doing when it came to her. God help me.

12

ALLIE

I was in panic mode and it had nothing to do with the jerkwad outside. It was Thorn. I'd let him pull me inside, away from everyone else. Just the two of us. Sure, I was a little taken aback by the fact that I could so easily break a bottle to use as a shank, but then again, I wasn't some delicate flower. I was capable enough to stop Thorn if I hadn't wanted to be alone with him. Yet here I was, facing a man whose sex appeal was something that should go down in the record books.

Thorn's eyes glowed in the dim light of the bar. He seemed bigger behind the bar, where there was less space, and I felt myself being tugged towards him by the sheer will of my body. I wanted him like I'd never wanted anyone or anything before in my life.

I knew the difference between right and wrong and I knew I shouldn't, but I couldn't help myself. Or, maybe I could and I just didn't want to anymore. The man made resisting him for twenty-four hours feel like a lifetime of neglect.

A strong hum from the music that someone had turned on over the loudspeakers outside teased me, an old southern rock beat pulsing in tune with my heartbeat until I could feel it all over my skin, in my core, at the tips of my breasts. I felt like I was in heat.

"I shouldn't do this..."

Thorn watched me with his lower lip caught between his teeth, while his eyes danced over my body and face. When he let his lip go, there were indentions from his teeth there that I wanted to lick. "Do what, Allie?"

"This...thing with us." I gestured between our bodies, my knuckles grazing his stomach as I did.

He reacted like I'd burned him. He sucked in a sharp breath and stood up taller. "Leave then. Get back out there and serve drinks. Do the smart thing for both of us."

I should, yessiree, I absolutely should. I stepped closer to him. "You want me to go?"

He stared over my head and grabbed the bar behind him. His knuckles were white from the grip he had on it. "Yeah. I think you should."

I didn't want to hear no from him. I didn't want to leave and be the good girl. I could maybe justify it later by rationalizing that I wanted the experience of being the one who did the bad thing for a change, but honestly, that had nothing to do with it. I just wanted Thorn with every screaming cell of my body. I wanted him inside of me. I wanted him to do things to me. Naughty things. Things that I'd never wanted another man to do. I needed him bad.

"Not happening." I leaned into him, pressing my chest against his, and gasped as my nipples met his solid body. His bare skin was hot to the touch and I couldn't wait to taste him. "Do you know that out of the four serious boyfriends I've had, all four of them have cheated on me?" I don't know why I said that. Maybe an attempt at justifying what I was about to do?

He tilted his head back and stared up at the ceiling, still not touching me. "Even the fiancé?"

I gave in and dipped my face forward so I could run my tongue up his chest. "Yep."

That gained me a low growl and I rewarded myself by moving over slightly and flicking my tongue over his nipple. The jerk and tensing of his muscles encouraged me so I did it again.

"Every single one of them," I whispered softly, "and I still remained the good girlfriend. Doting and caring. Baking goddamned cupcakes and showing up at their offices in nothing but a trench coat. I was an all-star friggin' girlfriend to each of them."

I raked my nails down from his shoulders and lightly bit down on his nipple before moving to the other one and doing the same. "Still kept right on smiling through the pain and doing my very best to not inconvenience anyone."

I turned around and snaked my body against Thorn's, wiggling until I felt his rock-hard boner pressing between my ass cheeks. When I straightened, I wrapped my arms behind me and around the back of his neck. "I'm done with that. I deserve to be bad. Help me be bad, Thorn."

I let out a squeal as he grabbed me and spun me around so that I was sitting on the work station in front of him, his hands branding my knees where he touched them.

"You want to be bad?"

I bit my lip and nodded.

"Take off your shirt."

I sucked in a sharp breath and slowly moved my hands to the hem of my shirt. "Just this one time, Hawthorn. Just enough to get it out of our systems."

He stepped back so that no part of him was touching me and then crossed his arms over his chest. "Shirt, Allie. Take it off. No talking."

My pulse soared. Not knowing what he was thinking was like holding my hand over a flame. It set me on fire, the danger so real and threatening to the life I'd accepted for myself. Would he grab me on my way out of work the next day and demand a replay? The day after that? My one-time rule would probably be dependent on how well Thorn adhered to it. I already knew I was too weak to say no to him.

I pulled my shirt off and then hesitated. Did he want the bra, too?

"Take it off."

I undid the front clasp and straightened. I had to rake in all the confidence I possessed to release the cups and sit there, completely exposed, in front of the hottest man I'd ever laid eyes on. His reaction to seeing my bare breasts tumble out took away any doubts I had.

Thorn growled and slammed his hands on the metal station, on either side of my thighs. His eyes remained riveted to my chest, glowing as he licked his lips. "Fucking idiots."

I leaned away from him. "Excuse me?"

"The boyfriends. Fucking idiots. What kind of man could experience *your* tits and still wander?"

I laughed but it turned into a cry of pleasure as he leaned forward and nipped the top of my right breast. I caught his head in my hands and pulled him up to my mouth. "More."

He shoved my knees apart and stepped into the gap there. With one hand, he dragged me closer to the edge, so his erection rubbed against my panty clad core, and with the other hand, he grabbed my hair and used it to tilt my head to the side so he could devour my mouth in a soul-shattering kiss.

I never stood a chance when it came to denying Thorn Canton.

13

HAWTHORNE

I was fucked. One taste of her peaches and cream skin and I was a lost man. I still had all these ideas and convictions in my head about staying away from her and not wanting a mate, but all it took was one taste of the tip of her perfect breast to make me crumble like a slobbering idiot. I thought I could turn my craving for her off and on like a switch, but it didn't seem to be working out that way.

I took her mouth, kissing her like I'd die if I didn't. She tasted like whiskey and sugar, as sweet as she was spicy. I slid my tongue against hers and rocked my dick against her wet panties. Her smell surrounded me, arousal and her natural scent, until every breath I took in was a piece of her.

She sucked my bottom lip between her teeth and bit it before flicking her tongue over it. "Fuck me, Thorn."

I jerked against her, hot blood rushing away from my brain at an alarming rate. I'd never been so hard. "You're killing me, woman."

She locked her legs around my ass and pulled me harder against her. "I feel like I'm going crazy. I just want to feel you in me."

I kissed down her jaw and brushed my teeth against her throat and neck, leaving a trail of goosebumps behind. "Wait."

She writhed against me. "Don't want to."

I cupped her perfect tits in my hands and tweaked her light pink nipples before lowering my mouth and taking them in, one at a time. "You put me in charge, baby. You're going to have to do what I say."

She shivered under me and yanked harder on my hair. "Mistake. I'm taking charge. Fuck me now."

God, I was going to shoot a load into my pants if she kept talking like that. Instead of listening to her, I kissed farther down. I dipped my tongue into her navel and then moved even lower. I buried my face into her lap and rubbed her through her skirt with my nose and chin. "I'm going to taste your pussy until you come for me first."

The wrecked cry that fell from her lips had me clenching my whole body. I flipped her skirt up and then easily yanked the lace panties down her legs. I caught her ankles in my hands and stroked up her legs until I had the bottom of her thighs in my palms. Her skin was soft and supple, her curvy legs delicious looking as I lifted them and rested them on my shoulders.

Allie leaned back, her elbows on the bar, eyes burning me. Her soft hair was splayed across the bar, the ends falling off the other side. The picture of her spread out before me brought out an unexpected roar from deep within me. My bear was pleased.

Instead of reacting with judgment of any kind to my roar, Allie wiggled her hips under my face. Her wild and free scent was even stronger there and I couldn't help but devour her. I buried my face in her and used my tongue to fuck her. Long strokes followed by focused flicks of my tongue on her clit, I worked to make sure my mate was pleased. When she shook under me, I moved my mouth lower and rocked it into her, I wanted to make her cry out in pleasure.

She made me feel like I'd hooked myself up to an electric current. Tasting her sweetness, feeling her luscious curves, hearing her soft moans, I was held back by barely a thread from standing up and slamming my dick home in her.

"Thorn!" Her voice broke and I glanced up to see the pure pleasure on her face.

I growled into her core and grinned when more wetness leaked out of her shivering body. I slid two fingers into her and caught her clit in my mouth as she bucked her hips.

Allie's walls tightened around my fingers as she came undone under me. I kept my mouth on her until she went limp and still stayed where I was, licking her slowly and watching her shudder. Her body was mine. I rubbed my face against her thighs, marking her with my scent. Hers would be all over me and I couldn't stop the possessiveness taking over. I wanted anyone close to her to know that she was mine.

I hooked my arms behind Allie's back and easily pulled her up. Her eyes were still half-closed and a smile of satisfaction graced her face. "Beautiful." The word just escaped my lips without thinking. But she was. The way she looked right now in my arms, she was easily the most beautiful sight I'd ever seen.

She hooked her arms around my neck and swayed a little. "What did you do? I think I just melted."

I nudged her with my aching dick. "I'm not finished yet."

Her lips parted to say something but a sound came from the front door of the bar and I looked up and watched as the door started to swing open. Allie squeaked and jumped down from the work station. I stepped back to make room for her and snatched her bra off the bar at the last second.

I normally wouldn't give two shits about getting caught, but this felt different with Allie. I didn't want anyone else to see her, but I also didn't want people in the bar talking about her like she was some easy hook up. "Stay down. I'll get rid of 'em. Then, we'll finish this."

Curiously, she didn't bother putting on her shirt or bra. She stayed kneeling in front of me, her eyes on mine as we waited for whoever was interrupting us to leave. It made me hotter than hell to know that she wasn't done, either. The image of her on her knees in front of me was also going to top my spank bank from now on.

"You aren't playing today, Thorn?"

I jerked my eyes up to see George Vaughn coming in. Thank God, he was a human and wouldn't be able to scent that Allie was behind the bar with me. "Not yet. I came in here to finish some stuff up before heading back out there. What can I do for you, George?"

Allie's hands moved to my ass and then pulled my shorts down before I could stop her. I let out a startled sound and leaned forward so George wouldn't be able to see that I was naked. I felt the shocking heat of her lips on the head of my engorged cock and the breath seized in my lungs.

"I was hoping I could bother someone for a couple of shots of whiskey. Martha has me cutting back on the beer, so I can't have any outside where she's watching. You know how women are."

Allie's teeth lightly scraped me as she opened her mouth and took as much of me in as she could. Her hot mouth closed and then she pulled back with the most amazing suction I'd ever felt.

"She, uh, she lets you have whiskey?" I sounded like I was in pain, but hopefully George would let it go. I had to get rid of him so I could punish the little hellcat at my feet for the game she was playing.

"No, but what she doesn't know won't hurt her, right?" He laughed. "I didn't see a problem with the beer. It's not like I'm drinking all day long or anything..."

I lost track of what the older man was saying as Allie cupped my balls and surprised me by taking my full length down her throat. She sucked in long and hard strokes before licking just the head like it was her favorite lollipop. I was close to losing it. George had to get the hell out.

14

HAWTHORNE

"George!" I shook my head and winced. "Uh, sorry. Here, take the bottle."

"Wow! You're sure? The whole bottle?"

I reached down and grabbed a fistful of Allie's hair to pull her mouth off of me. I was seconds from coming. "Yep. See you later."

"You okay, Thorn? You look a little flushed."

Allie wrapped her fist around my dick and squeezed. I jerked forward, bumping her mouth and putting myself close enough that she could lick me again.

With a loud groan, I pulled harder on her hair to keep her away from me. "I'm fine. Bye, George."

The old man gave me a look but turned away. I was a man possessed. If George turned back around, he was going to get an eyeful, because before the door even closed, I had Allie up and bent over the work station, with the tip of my dick pressing against her glistening folds.

Wet heat welcomed me like a glove and Allie arched her back and tried to work her hips back so I would slide in farther. She looked at me over her shoulder, her hair wild from my hands, eyes half-mast, and licked her lips. "I need you, Thorn."

I grabbed both of her ass cheeks and squeezed, lifting her curvy body higher. Seeing her bent over like that was better than I'd imagined. Her ass curved perfectly under my hands. She was standing on her toes and wiggling, begging me with her body for what she needed. I needed it, too. I wanted to taste her once more, though. I wanted to hear her really beg me for it. I wanted to know that when it was over she couldn't say that she hadn't been desperate for me.

I knelt behind her and spread her open from behind, the way I'd wanted to from the first moment I saw her ass. She let out a startled cry as I pushed my face against her body and tasted her again, dragging my tongue in one long lick that elicited a gasp. Again and again I licked what was mine as her body quivered with pleasure.

It seemed like I'd barely started when she came again and then slapped her hands against the bar top. "Please! Thorn, I need to feel you in me. I'm begging you!"

That's what I wanted to hear. I stood up and playfully slapped her ass. "I could eat you for breakfast, lunch, and dinner, Allie. You taste like heaven."

She moaned as I lined our bodies up. "One time."

I pushed into her tight body and squeezed her hips, feeling my control slip. There was no way it would just be one time. It was too good. One time would never be enough. Halfway in and I felt her pulse around me. She was so damn tight that it was almost too much. I was too close, too soon.

I ran my hands up her smooth back and then wrapped my hands in her hair. "Hold on, baby."

She cried out my name as I thrust the rest of the way into her. Her body clenched around me and then she dropped her head and let it hit the bar. "Good lord. Fuck me, Thorn. Why is this so good?"

I pulled her head back and lifted her waist so she was pinned against the station with her back against my chest. I cupped her perfect titties and licked from her shoulder to her ear. "This isn't a one-time thing."

She turned her head and found my lips with her own. The kiss was heated, a battle of control, but when I slowly pulled out of her and then thrust back in hard, her lips parted in an "o". I kissed down her throat and then bit down on the skin at her shoulder, torturing her and myself. My bear roared, demanded I mark her, but I couldn't. Not like this. Instead, I focused on where we were joined. I wanted her to feel me the next day.

I lost myself in her. I held her against my chest, thrusting in and out of her until I felt my body tightening. Allie rolled her hips against me and moaned loud enough to damn near alert the whole town as she got closer to another orgasm. She held my arms where they latched around her and dug her nails in my skin as my thrusting grew erratic.

"Oh, God, Thorn..."

I lowered my hand and circled her clit with the pad of my finger as I teetered on the edge. I wanted her to come with me.

Instantly, her body tightened and she tossed her head back. Her lips parted in a scream that I desperately wanted to hear and then the sweetest sound came from her mouth, the sound I'd needed to hear. My name on her lips, broken from pleasure, screamed loud enough for someone to hear all the way in Dallas.

She was mine.

I came harder than I've ever come in my life, pulsing jets of my seed filling her as I held her while we both gasped for air. It didn't feel like it'd ever stop. Even when I could breathe evenly again, the pull to her, the pleasure, the awareness was overwhelming.

I let go of her hair and ran my hand down her back, enjoying the tremors that made her body clench. "More than one time."

She looked back at me with the sexiest expression of complete satisfaction. "You don't like boundaries, do you?"

I laughed and stroked my hand over her ass. "Not even a little bit. Not with you, especially."

"Too bad. It was still a one-time thing." She reached back and gently pushed me away.

I slid out of her painfully slowly, dragging out another moan from both of us. I was amazingly still hard and could go again, if she wasn't determined to keep me away. "How about we-"

"Oh, God!" Allie turned to face me, shock and horror frozen all over her face. "We didn't use a condom."

I looked down at my bare cock, still wet from our combined fluids, and winced. It hadn't occurred to me. She was my mate. Somewhere in the middle of screwing her brains out, my mind had decided that it was okay because she was mine. Looking at it with a clear head, I could understand where she was coming from, why she was freaking out...

"Oh, shit."

She bent over and grabbed her shirt and bra, hastily pulling them on while moving away from me. "This is why I don't do things like this. What the hell was I thinking? This was a mistake."

Ouch. Mistake. Her words felt like a dagger to the heart. I jerked my pants up and moved to touch her, but she yanked away from me.

She whirled around and nailed me in the face with the shirt I'd given her earlier. "I'm going home. I can't do this."

"Home?"

"To the trailer! Just leave me alone, Thorn." Already halfway across the bar, she muttered to herself. "I'm such a fucking idiot."

I watched her go and then slammed my fists down on the bar, cracking the wood straight down the middle from side to side. "Dammit!"

15

ALLIE

The trailer was too small for the pacing I needed to do. I needed something closer to the size of a football field if I was going to really pace my restless energy out. As it was, I was just making tight circles between the bed and the kitchenette. Tight circles with my legs spread slightly too wide to be considered normal.

I was wickedly sore, every swipe of my jogging pants brushing against my panties reminded me of just what I'd done. My body was a traitorous whore. It didn't care that my mind was in a bad way. It just wanted Thorn back inside of it.

I wasn't so completely panicked that I didn't understand. Thorn had managed to give me not only multiple orgasms for the first time ever, but the strongest, most earth-shattering orgasm of my life. I was wrecked. I thought I could do it. I thought I could sleep with him once to experience it and to get past the sexual tension between us, but it wasn't that easy for me. I'd just ended up making an even bigger mess for myself.

I couldn't stop thinking about how I'd never once felt as connected to Eric in the years that I'd been with him as I did to

Thorn in the *day* that I'd known him. Eric had never given me multiple orgasms. Eric had barely given me orgasms at all.

It didn't make sense. I shouldn't have these kinds of feelings towards Thorn. I didn't know him. I'd barely talked to him. Yet, there was something deep and all-consuming there. Just like with Burden and the bar. I should've been freaked out by the massive sense of déjà vu, but instead, it was comfortable. Well, not with Thorn, but the bar and town felt comfortable. Thorn was all danger, all the time. If I knew what was good for me, I'd stay away from him. That was, if I hadn't managed to massively fuck up. I couldn't believe I hadn't used protection. It was obvious he slept around. A lot. *A player, for God's sake, Allie!*

What if he had something? What if he'd given me an STD? I was a fool for making that mistake. I couldn't even begin to let myself panic about the prospect of pregnancy. I just had to believe that pregnancy wasn't even an option.

I'd been alone in the trailer for a few hours, pacing and driving myself bat-guano crazy, mostly because of Thorn, but also because Kayla had stopped by with her phone charger. She told me to keep it for the night and my phone was on the kitchen table, charged. The thing was like a monster, lying in wait, crouched to pounce and devour me alive. I was almost afraid to touch it.

It was stupid, but I didn't want to face Eric. I had issues, and for some reason, he was one I had the hardest time dealing with. Eric was far from perfect, despite his belief that he was God's gift to women. What I'd told Thorn was real. Eric had cheated on me in the beginning of our relationship and again several months ago. Probably a few times in between, if I were being honest with myself. Each time was a crushing blow. Yet, I'd stayed. Even though I was in pieces on the inside, I'd stayed. It was normal for me, I guess, given the example I'd had.

Before my parents passed, my father had been a habitual cheater and my mother, a habitual turn the other way-er. She'd always made it work. It'd seemed like they loved each other. They acted happy, at least. It wasn't until I was older, and looked back at my parents through different eyes, I realized that Mom had spent nearly all her time locked in her room. She wasn't happy. Somehow, even knowing that and knowing that allowing a man to cheat on you was wrong, I couldn't seem to stop landing in the same situations.

Every one of my serious boyfriends cheated. Even though Eric cheated, I rationalized, he still treated me pretty well and wanted to give me the world. I suppose I felt like I'd never find a guy who didn't cheat, so why not just accept the one who also wanted to take care of me.

Yet, when it came down to it, I'd frozen. When facing the prospect of actually tying myself to Eric, to a man who cheated, I couldn't commit. It'd felt like I was tying a brick to my ankle and jumping into the ocean. Panic had clawed its way up my chest until I thought I would choke to death, right there in front of him. Apparently, some part of me was salvageable and knew that I didn't deserve that life, that I shouldn't commit myself to my mother's fate.

Instead of facing that truth, though, I ran. I grabbed whatever clothes I had at his house and jumped in my car and fled the scene. I didn't quit my job, I didn't tell him I was leaving the state until I was miles over the border. I didn't even tell my friends goodbye. I just got out of there. I think a part of me thought that I was as weak as my mom, and that I'd fall into the same trap she did if I didn't run. That's why I was terrified to turn my phone on and see what was happening in Eric's world.

I also had to face the fact that I'd allowed myself to cheat. I was ashamed of how much I'd enjoyed myself and how little I cared about Eric while doing it. Was that how it had been for him?

A heavy knock sounded on the door and I jumped. "Yeah?"

"It's me, Allie." Thorn's deep as sin voice called through the door. "I came to check on you."

I looked down at my stained jogging pants and worn T-shirt. I wasn't dressed for company, that was for sure. I also wasn't supposed to be worried about what he thought of my outfit. I took a step closer to the door and then backed away. I wasn't sure what to do.

"I can hear your mind working from here. I just want to talk. Come out here and I'll keep my hands to myself."

"What do you want to talk about?"

He chuckled. "Stuff. Come out."

I pulled on a jacket and opened the door. He was already sitting on the tailgate of his truck, several feet away. I shut the door behind me and sauntered over to him, feeling the awkwardness grow with every step. I'd just washed him off my body a few hours earlier.

"Hey."

I stood a few feet away and nodded. "Hi."

"Come, sit down."

I shook my head. Like I needed any more temptation than what he already presented. "I'm good here."

Thorn had changed into jeans and a worn flannel. His hair was still damp and he smelled frickin' delicious. His eyes were heated as they looked me over, but he kept his hands on his thighs. "I'm sorry about earlier, Allie. I just...lost control of myself."

I hadn't been expecting an apology. I shifted my weight to my other foot and sighed. "It was just as much my fault as it was yours. I don't know what came over me."

He raised an eyebrow. "Really?"

My body heated. "Shut up. I didn't mean it like that. I just... I've never been that careless."

Thorn sighed. "Me either."

I huffed out a laugh, thinking it'd been a joke. When he gave me an annoyed look, I frowned. "You don't...do that? I mean, you don't have unprotected sex?"

"I can honestly say that you're the first person I've ever slipped up and not used a condom with. With a past like mine, you don't mess up stuff like that."

"Until you do..." I moved closer to him and pulled my sleeves over my hands nervously.

"What do you mean, with a past like yours?"

16

HAWTHORNE

I wanted to grab Allie and pull her into my chest. The overwhelming feeling of needing to hold her was as intense as it was new. She looked sexy as hell with her pajamas and her damp hair piled on top of her head. She'd even put on glasses at some point. Soft and welcoming, like a big green light, asking me to scoop her up and cradle her in my arms.

I didn't know what to do with those feelings, though. I was still fighting the urge to run away. I had no fucking clue what I was doing sitting outside of the trailer, begging her to talk to me. I never talked to women like I was about to talk to her. I never even talked to the guys about shit like this.

"Hawthorne?"

I nodded to the tailgate and smiled. "Sit with me and I'll tell you."

She stared at the spot and then at me. "No touching."

Like hell. "Sure. No touching. Just come up here."

"Fine." She climbed up and sat cross-legged, facing the trailer. "Now, talk."

I swallowed. "Well, to give you a little background about the town of Burden, the original families have a slightly interesting history."

She pushed her glasses up on her nose as she stared. "Yeah?"

I told her the story, leaving a few key details out. "Native Americans lived on this land. Our ancestors, *my* ancestors, were Native American. The legends say that when our gods were creating the earth, after they had put all the other mountains down, they ended up around here with a handful left, so they just dropped them all in Big Bend. Then, they knew that the land would be too rugged for normal people, so they moved us here."

I paused, the rest of the story was that they'd needed tougher beings than humans, and bear shifters were born. Over time the land got easier and our bear ancestors found human mates and settled farther north of Big Bend. I didn't think she was ready to hear that part yet, though.

"Our ancestors believed in soulmates. They believed that the gods made one other being on this planet just for them. It's a belief that our families passed down from generation to generation and it's still relevant today."

She looked up at me, her eyes large and innocent on her face. "Do you believe that, too?"

God. I wanted more than anything to tell her. If I did, it would mean either one of two things. She'd think I was crazy or disgusting and high-tail it out of Burden, or she'd want to settle down with me and start popping out kids. I damned sure wasn't prepared for either of those things. I was in a quandary that felt a little like quicksand. "I don't know what I believe. I didn't exactly have the best example of it.

"My mom was a little wilder than anyone expected her to be. She wasn't smart about it and ended up getting knocked up by Tommy Graham, the town drunk. Tommy Graham, my father. Three months later, she met the man who was meant to be her soulmate. He stayed with her, even though he was repulsed by me. He hated the constant reminder of her past. Me. Despite being meant for her, he couldn't take it. Ran off in the middle of the night when I was eight. Didn't take long for Mom to go completely insane."

I shook my head and grunted, simplified it as much as I could.

"So, see? Unprotected sex resulted in a horrible mistake that ruined my Mom's life. No, I don't make that mistake... until I did."

Allie raised up a little higher and gestured with her hands. "That's bullshit."

I frowned. "What?"

"It's bullshit. Unprotected sex got your Mom a baby boy, not a mistake. I'm sure you were a beautiful baby, too. Just look at you." Her cheeks reddened but she continued. "A weak man who couldn't accept that his lady wasn't innocent as a baby lamb when she came into his bedroom ruined your Mom's life. No good man would've turned his back on the love of his life because she had a child with another man."

"You feel strongly about that, huh?"

"Yes. Obviously, unprotected sex isn't *always* a mistake." She said it and then paused. Her face flamed even brighter and she waved her hands around. "That's not what I meant. I don't mean us. We definitely shouldn't have had unprotected sex. We should be more careful. *Should've* been more careful!"

I laughed.

She blew out a rough breath. "That was a train wreck. What I meant is that I don't think you were a horrible mistake. You were meant to be here."

"Thank you." I tugged lightly at a strand of hair she'd missed and smiled at her. "So, what about your parents? Got any legends or prophecies?"

"Um, only if you count the fact that I'm destined to end up with someone who cheats on me." Allie crossed her arms and rolled her eyes. "Dad was a cheater. A big one. Everyone in town knew about it. Mom knew. I knew. She pretended to be so happy, though. He'd come waltzing in at seven in the morning, smelling like liquor and cheap perfume and she'd smile and ask him if he'd like his eggs fried or scrambled. Every day."

I felt an ache in my chest. "What'd he say?"

"Scrambled. Every time."

"So, you grew up thinking it was normal for a man to be a cheating pig."

"Yeah. By the time I realized Mom had, in fact, been miserable all those years, and my parents didn't have the perfect marriage, it was too late. I was already entrenched in a pattern of finding men who don't care enough to be faithful and Mom and Dad were gone."

She tilted her head back and looked up at the stars. "They died in a car accident. The officer who worked the scene said that Dad lost control of the car and hit a truck head on. Later on, I found out that they'd been fighting in a bar. She'd shown up and confronted him. He'd drank too much, and heading home, swerved into the truck. The one time she tried to fight for herself, she ended up in a body bag on the side of the road stretched out somewhere between Joe's Tavern and the local Tastee-Freeze. What a way to go."

She abruptly stood up and paced a little circle in front of me. "Where's your mom? You said she went insane, but what happened then?"

I sucked in a harsh breath, realizing that I'd stopped breathing while she spoke. "Gone."

"And your dad?"

"Died somewhere in California. Passed out in a puddle of his own vomit."

When she looked at me again, there were tears in her eyes. "How do you know when someone's your soulmate, Thorn? Is there some kind of sign?"

"Allie..."

"How do you know, Thorn?"

"There's supposedly a magic to it, although some call it instinct, chemistry, whatever. An undeniable attraction and need for the other person. You're just supposed to know." I spit the words out and held her wide-eyed gaze.

Allie stood, frozen, in front of me. Her eyes narrowed. I could see the wheels turning in her head and I was terrified of the conclusion she was coming to.

A flash of pain washed over her face momentarily contorting her features, and then she took a step back. "I see..." she mumbled. "I'm going to head to bed. I'll see you later, Thorn."

I stood up. "Wait, Allie..."

She didn't, though. She hurried inside and the sound of the lock turning after she shut the door was deafening. My bear demanded that I chase her down and let her know that we weren't rejecting her. I couldn't, though. I wouldn't go after her. I wouldn't let this happen.

17

ALLIE

I was losing it. Listening to Thorn talk about his ancestors and sitting under the stars had left me with a million questions buzzing in all directions in my brain like flies circling a honey jar. All began with 'what if'. I abruptly ended the conversation with Thorn because I had suddenly had the overwhelming feeling that what he was telling me was that he was my soulmate but that he didn't want to be.

I glanced up at my reflection in the bathroom mirror and gave myself a look. "Soulmate? Really?"

The stuff he'd been saying, about just knowing and there being this insane attraction and connection, it just went straight to my head. One minute we were spilling our guts and the next, I was looking at him like he was some sort of magical, mystical creature of legend and folklore. My soulmate. It was stupid, but I couldn't control the desperate feeling of finally finding that deep connection. Surely, a soulmate wouldn't cheat. But I was being ridiculous. Thorn couldn't even say it with a straight face. Each time he'd said the word soulmate, he'd winced. There was no way we were soulmates. Unless life hated me.

I shook my head and spit out the toothpaste in my mouth. "Just forget about it, Allie."

I'd let the day get to me. I was probably delirious from all the orgasms my boss had given me. Leave it to me to think the first man who knew his way around my female anatomy was my soulmate. Pathetic.

I needed to be grounded. In a hurry. I grabbed my phone and climbed into bed before turning it on and dialing Eric. It was late enough in Burden and an hour later than that in North Carolina, but I knew he would be up.

"Alyson?" His slightly nasally voice hit me and my first thought was that it didn't send tingles through me the way Thorn's did.

"Hey. It's me."

"Good God, Alyson! It's been days since you called me. What the hell is going on? I've been worried sick."

I traced the outline of the ceiling with my eyes and frowned. "My phone died and I didn't have the charger. I'm sorry I worried you."

I heard the sound of his whiskey glass being put on the side table as he sat up. "Look, Allie, I've let you do this for long enough. You need to come home, now. Everyone's asking where you are and I don't know what to tell them. It's beginning to get awkward."

"I'm not ready to come home, yet."

"I don't care."

"Why did you cheat on me?" I asked the question before I even realized it had slipped out of my mouth. I wasn't sorry to have asked it, though. It was a question I should've asked much sooner.

"Let's not do this now, Alyson. I've got a big meeting with a potential client tomorrow. I'm talking a huge case. I score this job and we'll be honeymooning wherever you want, for as long as you want."

Honeymoon? I hadn't even accepted his proposal! "It hasn't phased you that I haven't said yes yet, has it?"

"We both know you're going to marry me. We can dispense with the formalities. You love me, Alyson. Just like I love you. Now, come home. Do you need me to say please or something?"

I sat up and rested my head between my knees. "Why do you want to be married to me?"

"What? Why are you mumbling?"

"I asked you why you want to be married to me."

There was silence and then I heard the distinctive *pop* of his favorite glass whiskey decanter being opened. "Why does anyone want to get married? It's just what people do, Allie. Where's all this coming from?"

"That's romantic. It's just what people do?" I sighed and fell back into my pillow. "I don't know about any of this anymore."

"Is that what you're asking for? You want romance? You want me to come home with flowers and write you fucking poetry? I'm a little too busy, honey. We're both long past adolescence."

"I'd probably find you keeping your dick in your pants a little romantic." *Did I just say that?*

He scoffed. "What is this all about? You're not being yourself at all. First, you run out of the house like a child, and now, this aggressiveness."

"Would you keep cheating on me into our marriage? Would it stay the same?"

"Of course not. For God's sake, Alyson, I've apologized. You need to let it go now."

I didn't believe him for one second and not just because I had the history to prove that cheaters never changed. "I don't want to marry you. It's actually the last thing I want to do."

"What?!"

"I don't want to marry you. I don't want to be married to a man who doesn't love me enough to be faithful to me. I was stupid to stay with you after the first time."

Eric remained silent, a tactic I knew he used to get me to cave in to what he wanted. I wasn't giving in, though. I refused to live the life my mother led. I wasn't going to waste my time on this Earth. Granted, Thorn probably wasn't my soulmate, and in fact, his story was probably just old folklore, but I liked the idea of having a soulmate who was made just for me.

"Is there someone else?"

I laughed, bitterly. "You can cheat, but I can't, huh? I'm sorry, Eric, but we're through. I should've ended this relationship the first time you cheated on me, but I didn't, so here it is. I deserve more than you. I deserve a... a... soulmate."

"What the hell, Allie? Soulmate? What are you on? You're just going to end a three-year relationship just like that? And over the phone? Don't be insane."

"If I forgot anything at your house, just get rid of it."

"Where are you? I'll come get you. Clearly you're not in your right mind right now."

I hung up and turned the phone off before he could call me back. Breaking up with him was unexpected, but it felt incredibly freeing. A weight had just been lifted from my shoulders. I stretched out on the bed and stared up at the ceiling. I didn't have to settle for a man who would cheat on me constantly. That was a choice, and from now on, I would be choosing differently. And maybe, just maybe, I would find someone who would treat me better than that.

18

HAWTHORNE

"What the fuck went down yesterday, man? The whole bar was a complete disaster last night." Hutch asked from his seat at Wyatt's mom's kitchen table. Sandra was outside, tending to her small greenhouse, and that was the only reason Hutch dared to mutter the *F*-word in her house.

I looked back towards the door to make sure she was still outside and shook my head. "I don't even know."

Wyatt leaned in. "The whole bar was so damn full of the scent of sex that Abram had to shut the place down. Nearly everyone in there was drunk as hell and trying to dry hump each other to kingdom come."

Sterling groaned and squirmed in his chair. "I think I broke my dick."

I raised my eyebrows. "What?"

"I took Kyle's little sister home last night. She waited until I got my pants off and then she punched me as hard as she could in the dick."

I shuddered. "You know that whole family hates you. Why did you even bother?"

"I had to try."

Hutch shook his head. "Dumb fuck."

"So, how was it? The way you disappeared last night, I figured you were going back for seconds right away."

I growled at Sam before I could stop myself. The silence that hung over the table was heavy and I swore. They had to know. No way would I ever get defensive over a casual hookup. "She's my fucking mate."

Sandra swept through the kitchen with a smack to the back of my head. "I don't care what she is. You curse like that again in my kitchen, Hawthorne Canton, and I won't hesitate to take a switch to you."

The woman had practically raised me and I winced under her glare. Sandra wasn't just Wyatt's mother, she was a mother to us all. "Yes, ma'am. Hutch said it first, though."

Wyatt snorted a laugh and it wasn't long before all hell broke loose. Sandra chased us out of her kitchen with her broom and we shifted and headed into the woods together, like we normally did after breakfast. We ran and shoved into each other, playing the same way we had since we were children. We'd been together for as long as any of us could remember and our bears reacted to each other like brothers.

When we'd worn ourselves out, we shifted back and dove into the lake at the back of Sandra's property. The water was ice cold and just what I needed to cool off.

"Your mate, huh?" Wyatt said it with a smirk that made me want to strangle him.

"Don't say anything. I know it isn't what any of us have ever dreamed of, settling down with one woman, but...fuck. My bear itches to be near her. And, she's not bad."

Wyatt rolled his eyes. "Not bad? Man, you've got to up your game with the compliments if you expect to keep her."

"She's already engaged. Plus, I'm not trying to keep her around. I'm not the settling down type. You know my history. I'll just fuck it up."

Hutch splashed me. "Brother, you don't get to pick when you're ready. It just happens. You can't fight it. Lucky bastard."

I looked around at them and frowned. "How would y'all feel if you were in my boots? Tell me you wouldn't be upset if you met your mate tomorrow and had to go directly to playing house?"

Wyatt shook his head. "Hell no I wouldn't be upset. A mate is a good thing, Thorn. Obviously, you had a different experience than us, but you can't think that what happened between your mom and stepdad is normal. It was fucked up. Super fucked up, and rare. It doesn't usually happen like that. You have as much chance as any other shifter to have a perfect mating."

I swam a few feet away, feeling uncomfortable with the topic. I couldn't help the doubts, though. "I thought you didn't want to find your mates, either. Aren't we all good like this? Bachelors playing the field, nothing to tie us down."

Sterling chuckled and shrugged. "I'd feel like I'd died and gone to heaven, bro. I'm not exactly holding my breath cause sometimes it doesn't happen and I don't want to jinx myself, but if my mate came along, I sure as hell wouldn't be here with you shitheads. I'd be with her, not letting her go."

Hutch nodded. "The idiot is right for a change. Any of us would give our right nut to find our mate. I would give up all other women for a mate in a heartbeat. Have you still had a wandering eye?"

I thought about it and sighed. "Naw. It's only been a little over a day, though."

"It won't change. You let her go and you'll spend forever yearning for her, never wanting another woman again."

I dunked myself and stayed under for as long as I could, trying to clear my head. I guess my parents' mating left a worse taste in my mouth than I realized. I'd just assumed the rest of the guys would be as disappointed as I was. Mating felt like a trap for me. The guys all acted like they'd be thrilled, but I wasn't sure yet. If I was being brutally honest with myself, I'd admit that I was scared as hell of what it meant for me. Watching Mom go fucking crazy had left scars that ran deep. I couldn't help imagining that happening to me. Or to Allie.

When I came back up to the surface, the guys were all swimming back to shore. Hutch looked over at me and sighed. "Don't fuck it up, man. You got what we'd all feel lucky as hell to get."

I stayed in the frigid water, my mind searching desperately for some sort of ease with the situation. I wanted to have the kind of confidence the guys had about having a mate. Instead, when I got out, I was pruned and no closer to finding peace.

19

ALLIE

T horn wasn't in the bar that night. His friends were all there, at their table, but when I brought a tray of drinks, no one mention him. They were acting pretty weird, too. Not even Sterling, who was the biggest flirt of the bunch, tried anything with me.

I focused on work and tried my best to ignore the strange gut-wrenching ache in my middle that had no business being there. Especially since I knew it had nothing to do with ending my relationship with Eric.

Abram gave me a look at the beginning of my shift, but didn't say anything about what I'd done with Thorn. I didn't know for sure that he knew, but I had this sixth sense that he did. It made me feel slightly awkward and weird the whole night. I couldn't tell if he was pissed at me or not and I hated it.

By the time we closed, I was exhausted. I'd run around the bar like a chicken with its head cut off all night long, covering for another server who'd called off. There was still no sign of Thorn and I was starting to get the message loud and clear. I thought of the expression on his face the night before. He'd gotten really freaked out when we had that discussion about soulmates.

Abram sat down at the bar and poured himself a glass of whiskey. "You want one?"

I shook my head and tossed my soiled towel into the bin with the others. "I'm good. Thank you, though. You okay, Abe?"

He met my eyes and a frowned etched his features into something that just didn't sit right on his usually jovial face. "You leaving?"

Taken aback, I made a face. "What? Are you getting rid of me?"

"No, of course not. I just figured, after what happened with Thorn, that you'd be running off."

I pressed my lips together and walked over to the jukebox to gather myself a moment. I suddenly felt like I'd disappointed my dad. "I'm sorry, Abram. I know you said to stay away and I tried... until I didn't."

"So, you *are* leaving?"

I moved back towards the bar and reached over it to pour myself a glass of the amber liquid. "No. I still don't have enough money to go anywhere. I'm also having some sort of early mid-life crisis. I broke up with my fiancé. Boyfriend, really. I never did accept the proposal."

Abram rested his hand on top of mine and smiled. "You fit in here. Wouldn't feel right if you left. Especially over Thorn, the big dumb jackass."

"Where is he, anyway? Does he normally avoid the bar, or is it me?"

"I don't know." When he saw my pointed look, he looked away and then groaned. "Probably you. He's an idiot."

He could say that again. I pushed off from the stool and grinned at him. "That's fine with me. It saves me the trouble, doesn't it?"

"I'm serious, Allie. I like him and he's a good guy, but he just doesn't know how to keep it in his pants for a girl. I don't think I've ever known him to actually *date* a girl."

I hated the ache in my chest but I forced a smile onto my face. "I didn't expect anything, Abram. You don't have to protect me. Now, unless there's anything else for me to do, I want to get back to the trailer and warm my toes in front of the space heater."

"Go ahead." He waited until I was almost out of the front door before talking again. "And Allie? I'm sorry about your almost fiancé. It's never easy to end something like that. Let me know if you need a day off or anything."

That time, my smile was real. "Thanks, Abram. I'm good, though. He was a jerk. I deserve better."

"You sure do."

I WALKED BACK to the trailer and locked myself in for the night, determined to just push through the feeling of rejection that was threatening to overpower me. Thorn was avoiding me. He was actually avoiding me like I was some clinger who would beg him for affection, or something. He didn't know me. I might've taken less than I deserved from exes, but I never begged anyone to stay and I sure as hell wasn't going to start with Thorn.

THE NEXT NIGHT I got to the bar and once again Thorn was conspicuously absent. He was seriously avoiding me. His friends' looks progressed to pity and I felt like karate kicking a hole in Thorn.

I walked up to their table and leaned down. "You can tell your yellow-bellied BFF that he doesn't have to hide from me. I don't want him anymore than I want herpes. Now, what do ya'll want to drink?"

Hutch's eyes widened and he bit down on his hand to keep from laughing. When he was composed again, he just nodded. "The usual."

I looked at the rest of them, in turn, with raised eyebrows, daring them to say something. My mood had gone from bad to worse in the wake of Thorn's continued cowardice. "I'll get that right out to you, boys."

The night progressed in pretty much the same way. I was miserably angry and kept picturing Thorn's face with a bullseye transposed over top. I may have crossed the line into obsession, but I couldn't stop thinking about him. If I wasn't thinking about knocking him out,

I was thinking about how he'd taken me on the bar. Or, I was thinking about the fact that he was probably with some other woman right now. Knowing his type, I seriously doubted he'd slow down his prowess just because he and I had an intense hook up followed by a conversation about soulmates.

Abram, sensing my mood, told me to take tomorrow night off work and instead just come in for some fun. I figured I'd take him up on that offer because fun was exactly what I needed. I was single and ready to get out of the funk that Thorn Canton had put me in.

Maybe I needed a little support, too. Girl talk might help clear my head and I was seriously missing all my girlfriends from back home. When I got back to the trailer, I turned my phone back on and dialed Georgia.

Georgia Child and I had been friends since we were young schoolgirls and she was never far from her phone. She answered on the second ring, her voice distance as she spoke to someone in the background. "Well, what the hell was I supposed to do with it? Should I have folded it and put it next to the damn towels?!"

"Georgia?"

"Allie?!" She lowered her voice and I heard a door slam shut. "Holy shit, girl. Where have you been?"

"It's a long story. I miss you."

"I miss you, too. You missed Helen's birthday party. We hired a stripper and he turned up wearing a three piece, powder blue suit. He was also sixty."

I laughed. "I haven't been gone that long. Why didn't I know there was going to be a party for her?"

"It was last minute, hence the geriatric stripper." Rustling noises filled the phone and then she yelled more. "I'm on the phone, dickweed! Why don't you just get out of here?"

"Who is that? I thought you broke up with Steve?"

"I did. That's a new guy." She raised her voice. "He's leaving my life now, though, so there's nothing to tell!"

"I have some things to tell you, though. And I need some advice."

"You're pregnant, aren't you? Is that why you left? I wouldn't want to raise a child with that imbecile, Eric, either."

"No! It's not that, but..."

20

HAWTHORNE

"It's about fucking time you showed up around here. This isn't my bar, you overgrown cub. It's yours. You can't skip out on things for two days in a row because you're hiding from Allie. You're a grown man, Thorn. You sleep with someone, you man up and deal with it. I would've thought you'd be used to it by now, in a town this size."

My heart sped up and my palms grew sweaty. Sure as hell didn't feel like a grown man. "Is she here?"

He slammed a beer down, not paying any attention to the man who'd ordered it as it sloshed over the side and soaked the bar napkin. "I gave her the night off."

I looked around at the bar. It was still early and there weren't many patrons yet. It would pick up soon and then I'd be surrounded by smells and sounds. Maybe then, I'd be able to get her scent out of my head. It was everywhere. I didn't just smell her behind the bar, either, I could still smell her arousal if I breathed in deep, and my bear was going nuts.

I'd locked myself away for the past two days, in hopes of getting control of myself, and over my bear. I'd somehow managed to go from zero to I-can't-live-without-you over a woman I barely even knew. It just didn't seem smart or safe.

Safe. What a fucking four letter word. I was the guy who never worried about anything. I went out on a limb all the time. I took chances. Yet, when it came to Allie, I was a shitless coward. Would I ever be safe again? I hadn't even shifted the whole time I was hiding afraid that my bear would take over and run right to her.

Jesus, I'd lost my balls since she walked into town. No one else got it, either. To them, I was just being a fool. They talked about how they wouldn't miss a single second with their mate, but they didn't get it. They hadn't gone through the things I had, or seen what I'd seen. I had every right to want to protect myself from Momma's fate.

None of that made Abram talking to me like I was a fucking kid feel any better, though. I snarled at him and grabbed the beer he'd just opened before stomping off to my table. I was in a rare mood. I wanted to fight. I wanted to find someone who was willing to challenge me and I wanted to make them bleed. Hell, I wanted to rip their fucking head off. That was, if Allie stayed away. It'd be a shame to be in the middle of the fight and then go into scared kitty cat mode because she was headed my way.

If it was even possible, I swore I could feel her anger like a tangible thing and it brought me to my knees. The bond between us had already grown that strong.

I groaned and sank into my favorite chair. My back and legs were stiff from working out nearly all day long for two days. I'd thought that maybe a good workout would burn some of the excess energy off, but instead, I was just stiff and still eager to run to Allie.

A few minutes later, Hutch and Sterling showed up. Half an hour after that, Sam and Wyatt joined us. We tossed back a few beers and then moved on to whiskey as the place filled up.

"At least you're out of hiding, Thorn. We've missed seeing you in here."

Hutch slapped the back of Sam's head. "Really? We've missed him? For a bear, you sure are a-"

"Trouble. Kyle just walked in with his cute as hell little sister."

Sterling said it with an easy grin on his face, but I could feel the tension rolling off him in waves.

I felt my body readying itself for a fight and shrugged. "He wants to brawl, he knows where to find us. I, for one, am fucking ready."

Sterling swore. "And it just keeps on coming. Red alert, boys. Allie just walked in and she's looking to start her own fight, it seems."

I breathed in and her scent hit me like a brick to the face. Freedom, sunshine, and wild flowers. I felt her eyes land on my back and then her smell grew stronger. She was coming my way.

Hutch grimaced and sat back in his chair. "Here it comes."

"Fuck your life, brother." Sam pushed back from the chair, just in case he needed a quick exit. Chicken shit.

Allie stopped next to me and when I looked up, there was a smile curling her painted red lips. It didn't reach her smoky eyes, though, and I could feel the anger emanating from her. "It's good to see you back at work, boss. Hope whatever you had isn't contagious."

Before I could reply to her, she tilted her head, made a face at me like she'd smelled something she didn't like, and then turned and headed across the room. With ease, she sat down at a table of women who greeted her fondly. I recognized at least a few of my past hookups.

Wyatt whistled. "Damn. She's hot as hell when she's mad. That little dress ain't half bad to look at, either."

Before I knew what I was doing, I had the collar of his shirt bunched in my hands and I was growling in his face. I could feel my jaw starting to elongate with the shift, but I couldn't stop it right away. My bear was furious that he'd looked at our mate and I couldn't say that I wasn't just as pissed. "Keep your eyes to yourself, brother."

Wyatt grinned. "See. Look at that. You react to me just like a mate would. How about you react like a mate would to *her*?"

I jerked back into my own seat and scowled. "Not a funny trick, Wyatt. My bear wanted to rip your head off."

He shrugged. "I could take your bear any day."

My skin bristled and I squeezed my eyes shut. "Stop fucking challenging me, Wyatt."

"What are you going to do about it? Hide some more?"

I knew what he was doing. He was pushing me to act, but I wasn't going to. I bit my tongue hard enough to draw blood and leaned back in my chair, trying to appear relaxed. "Go bother someone else."

Sterling sat forward in his chair and laughed. "She isn't taking any prisoners tonight, boys. Hot da-yum."

I looked over and watched as Allie tossed down a couple of shots back to back. The arch of her neck as she tilted her head back and let the liquor roll down her throat, had me hard instantly. Her hair flowed freely down to the middle of her back and she casually raked a hand through it, flipping it from one side to the other. The curls teased me, touching her all over.

The red dress she wore was killer. Tight and fitted down her hips, then flowing freely around her thighs. It was another one that would blow up with a slight breeze and I wondered what color her panties were underneath.

Everything about her was calling me. I wanted to go to her and fuck her up against the bar again. My bear didn't care if everyone watched me mark her. He just wanted me to claim her as my own so the men in the bar would get the fucking hint. I needed to run, though. I needed to get the hell out of there so I didn't claim her without thinking. She'd made no promises to me. She didn't owe me staying in Burden. She could leave at the drop of a hat and let me rot away wallowing in my own shame and misery. Like my mother had.

Panic kept me in my chair. The guys talked around me, the music blared, people laughed. I barely breathed as I waited for a space to either calm down or run.

21

ALLIE

I 'd kept myself busy all day. After talking to Georgie for hours the night before, I woke up with a newfound determination to piss Thorn off. I went to the one and only salon in town and was able to get an appointment right away. I had my hair styled and then had them do my makeup. I still hadn't gotten around to purchasing any cosmetics, so it was different to be wearing it again. I felt sexy and confident.

I clicked with the women there and with a little prompting, very little, a few of us made plans to have a girls' night out. The Cave, of course, was the only place in town so, ta-da. Here we were, drinks in hand. Turned out that they were a little wild, and I loved it. I could feel Thorn across the room, itching to leave. I had to give him something to look at before he could slide out and make his escape.

I turned to Randi, the bubbly blonde next to me who'd styled my hair. "I'm going to dance."

"Not before you do a couple of shots, you're not!"

Shots magically appeared, delivered by Kayla with a wink. "Tip it back, pretty lady!"

I did as suggested and was met with a warmth taking over my

body and cheers from all the women around me. I slammed the shot glasses back on the table and stood up. "It's time!"

Samantha, the blonde I'd saved Thorn from my first night, bumped hips with me. "Tear up that dance floor!"

Very aware of the table across the room, the one with the large, angry looking boss-man, I slunk onto the dance floor and positioned myself where he could see me. Before I could even scan the male-heavy dance floor for a partner, a tall cowboy shimmied into the space in front of me and smiled.

"Mind if I have this dance?"

I smiled back at him and shook my head. "It'd be my pleasure."

An old country song was playing and the stranger wasted no time in slipping his arms around me and swaying us to the music. He smelled nice and he didn't stomp on my toes, so win-win in my book. When he spun me out and then curled me back into his side, I got the feeling he was going to kiss me, so I quickly spun myself back out and grinned. I wanted to infuriate Thorn, but I couldn't imagine my lips touching the stranger. Something about the thought repulsed me to my very core. I didn't understand it, because he was a good-looking man, but my body would have none of him.

I finished the song with him and then a faster song came on. He tipped his hat at me and let a younger guy cut in. I laughed as the new stranger shimmied his hips for me.

"These hips know how to move, little lady."

I laughed again, feeling the alcohol, and danced with him. I worked my hips too, hoping and praying that Thorn was affected by me. I could feel his eyes on my body and he was definitely having an effect on me. I felt slightly wild, swaying and moving.

Out of the corner of my eye, I saw Thorn grabbing a whiskey bottle from a passing waitress and blow out a frustrated breath. *Shit!* I wanted him going crazy with desire, not getting black out drunk. It didn't seem to matter what I wanted, however, because he pushed up his stupid John Deere hat, tilted his head back and took a long pull from the bottle.

Feeling angry beyond description, I pulled my stranger a little closer and wrapped my arms around his neck. "I love this song."

He nodded and brushed his cheek against mine when leaning in to whisper in my ear. "I don't want to give you the wrong idea, ma'am. I'm gay."

I snorted. "That is perfect. I'm trying to piss a man off. You against helping with that?"

He tugged me even closer and pressed his lips to my neck. "No, ma'am. Wait. Is he big enough to kick my ass?"

I winced and nodded. "Yeah. He's really big."

A careless shrug later and he captured my lips in a kiss that probably looked a lot hotter than it felt. When he pulled back, he pulled a card out of his pocket and made a show of slipping it into the cleavage of my dress. If a straight man would've done it, I would've knocked his block off.

"My name's Logan. That's my number. I'm going to head out so I don't get smashed by whatever hulk you're trying to piss off. Call me if you're ever in need of another beard. Or, just drinks. I'm up for either."

I let him kiss me again and then he slipped through the crowd, away from me. I couldn't help the silly grin on my face. I knew Thorn had watched the kiss. It was like I had a direct wave length to Thorn's emotions. They were volatile, for sure.

I danced by myself for a bit, winding my hips around and arching my back in a move I'd practiced as soon as I'd gotten my curves in when I was just hitting puberty. Samantha joined me with more shots and I was hard pressed to find a reason not to drink them.

The combined effects of all the drinks were starting to hit me hard when I sensed Thorn move. I knew he was headed my way, so I distanced myself from Samantha and the others. When he finally got through the crowd to me, he felt twice as big as normal. His eyes flashed and his smell seemed even more dangerous. It hit me from ten feet away, despite there being at least five other guys between us.

My heart sped up as I met his eyes and my back hit the wall

behind me. Thorn didn't stop coming until he was towering over me and I had to tip my head back to keep the eye contact.

"What do you think you're doing?"

The growl in his voice was like a tongue stroking my most private parts. I crossed my ankles and squeezed my thighs together. "I'm having a good time. What does it look like I'm doing?"

His eyes fluttered down to my legs and then back to my face. I watched as he took a deep breath in and then growled. He put his hands on the wall on either side of my head and narrowed his eyes at me. "You're playing with fire."

"What would you know about fire? You're too chicken-shit to get close to the heat. We both know you're going to run away again. Save me the trouble and go now, Thorn. Run."

He grabbed my arms and easily lifted me as if I weighed nothing. He only stopped when he could pin me to the wall with his rock-hard erection against my core. "You have no clue what you're getting into."

I couldn't look away from him. I didn't care if the entire bar was watching us. My body felt like it was going to explode under his touch. "So, tell me."

He suddenly dropped me and moved away. "It's better that you don't know."

I bore a hole through his back with my gaze as he strode away. The way my body reacted to his, the way I just knew what he was feeling... It was crazy, but that right there was the moment I knew. Thorn was without a doubt my soulmate. A concept that I hadn't even believed was real a couple of days ago, and couldn't explain in a way that didn't sound ridiculous, was now something I was convinced of with my whole heart. My soulmate was either a complete asshole or a giant idiot, though.

It was just my luck.

22

ALLIE

I sat at the bar for the next hour, nursing my wounded ego. I turned down a few offers to dance in favor of letting myself sit and mope. I wanted to find Thorn and kick his ass. He was being cryptic and weird, instead of just giving us a chance.

"Well, you don't look like you're using your day off to feel more relaxed." Abram slid a shot to me and watched as I took it. "What's your deal?"

I slumped on my stool. "I'm just going to say it. I'm going to say it, even if it sounds insane."

"Say what?"

"I think Thorn is my mate but he keeps running away from me."

Abram dropped a beer bottle he'd been opening and stared at me. "What did you say?"

I let my head fall onto the bar and groaned. "I told you it sounded insane. He told me about mates and I think he's mine. I'm his. I feel it with him and I know he feels it, too. He's being a pusscake, though. He won't face me for long enough to even have a conversation about it. He just keeps hiding or running away."

"He told you about mates?"

I nodded. "Yeah. He told me about his parents, too. I don't blame him for being scared, but I do blame him for being a coward."

Abram leaned across the bar and lowered his voice. "He told you about his parents?"

I made an exasperated sound. "Abram, keep up. He told me about soulmates and his parents."

"Holy shit. You are his mate."

I shook my head at Abram and turned on my barstool to look out at the crowd. A familiar face caught my attention and I gasped. "Oh, god! My boyfriend, I mean ex-boyfriend, just showed up! How the hell did he find me?"

"I thought you said you weren't running from him?"

"I'm not. I don't know why he's here. Shit. I'm sneaking out of the back. Make sure no one tells him where I'm staying." I snuck through the kitchen and let myself out the back door. I was slightly drunk and overly paranoid about Eric finding me, so I was extra wary of the door being loud. I made sure it silently shut and then turned around to map out my quickest route to the trailer.

Only, standing not ten feet from me was a huge bear carrying a bottle of Jack Daniels. Thank God it hadn't noticed me yet as it stumbled across the grass, swaying back and forth. It was grunting and making sounds that almost sounded like growly talking.

I watched on in horror as it tipped the bottle back, finishing the liquid, and then chucked it. The sound of glass shattering startled me out of my stupor with a slight squeak. I slapped my hand over my mouth and reached behind me with my free hand to try and get the back door open.

It was too late, though. The bear turned to me and I realized that at the top of its giant head sat a little John Deere cap. I screamed then, horrified at what it meant. Had the bear attacked Thorn? Had it... oh, God... eaten him? Stolen his hat? Drank his whiskey... okay that was weird. My heart felt like it was caving in as I thought of Thorn being eaten by a bear.

The bear waved its arms at me and I took a step backwards. It had oddly human movements as it headed over to attack and eat me, too.

With my back pressed against the door, I couldn't find the handle to let myself back in. I fumbled around searching, but when the bear stepped closer again, I froze. What was one supposed to do in the case of a bear attack? I thought it was make a lot of sound, but I didn't think my throat would allow anything else to come out.

The bear seemed to let out a massive sigh and then, in the blink of an eye, it was gone, and Thorn appeared. Naked. Holy moly, Thorn was naked as the day he was born and his downstairs waved in the cold night air, still large and seemingly leading the way.

"Shit, I'm sorry, Allie." He stepped closer, his hands out in front of him like he was approaching a scared dog. "I didn't mean for this to happen quite like that."

I stared up at his hat, still sitting on top of his head, like it hadn't just been on a bear's head. "What happened?"

He smelled like whiskey and man, and despite the situation, my body still responded to him. He tilted his head back and breathed in before closing the gap between us. His body pressed against mine and my breath caught in my throat.

"How can you still want me after what you just saw?"

"What exactly did I just see?"

The back door pushed against me as Eric's voice reached my ears. "Allie?! I heard you scream. Are you okay?"

Thorn swept me behind him and growled at Eric as he pushed his way blindly into the night. I could see him and his clean sweater and it was such a stark contradiction to Thorn's naked muscular form.

"What do you want?"

Eric moved to step around Thorn, but Thorn wasn't having it. Finally, Eric stopped and frowned up at him. "Why are you naked with my fiancé? Is he the reason you tried to break things off with me, Allie?"

"*You're* the fiancé?"

"What the hell is that supposed to mean? Of course, I'm the fiancé." Eric looked back at me and held out his hand. "Come on, Alyson. I'm taking you back home."

Still in shock, I backed away from both of them. I stepped on something slippery, and lost my balance. As I tumbled backwards, I heard Thorn cry out for me. Then a sharp pain burst at the back of my head and the night grew even darker.

23

HAWTHORNE

The little guy sitting across from me shivered in the chilly Texas night air. I couldn't help the predatory grin that curved my mouth. "Go on back home, boy. You'd probably do better in a warmer climate, huh?"

He scowled at me and stood up. "This is crazy. I'm going inside."

I unfolded my body from the lawn chair I'd been in for the past hour and stepped in front of the door. "You're not going inside. It's a small trailer. Doctor Mae said to wait out here."

"Look, I don't mean to be rude, but Alyson is going home with me. She and I... we've been together for a long time and a roll in the hay with some good ol' boy in hick-town, USA isn't going to change that."

I stepped closer to him and tried to remind myself that Allie would probably be upset if I ripped his limbs from his body. "I might've been hearing things funny, on account of my hick-town, good ol' boy hearing and all, but I thought you mentioned she broke things off with you. Did I hear that wrong or did she really dump your sorry ass?"

Eric had the good sense not to push it. He stumbled back to his seat and dropped into it. He wasn't all that small by normal standards, but next to me, he resembled a child. His pale blonde hair and pale skin didn't help his delicate appearance. I could see where she might consider him pleasant looking, but there was no way she was hot for that twerp.

"She's clearly confused. I don't know what's been happening here, but whatever it is, it's over now. She's going to come home with me where she belongs and she and I are going to work things out."

"She told me you cheated on her. What the fuck is wrong with you? You had the perfect woman and you stepped out?"

His cheeks turned red under the security light hooked up on the side of the trailer. "Our relationship is none of your concern. I'm done talking to you."

I sat back down and crossed my arms over my chest. I still hadn't bothered with finding a shirt. I'd pulled on my jeans, but my body temperature was up from the anger of seeing Eric. The cold wasn't touching me.

"Who are you, anyway?"

I glared at Eric. "Thought you were done talking to me?"

"I have a right to know who my fiancé has been running around with."

I tipped my head back and let my thoughts stray. Allie saw me shift. She hadn't said anything about it. She hadn't run, so that was something. Of course, right after that, she knocked herself unconscious.

I was a grade A moron for shifting so close to the bar. I'd just let the panic get to me. And the whiskey. I owed the bar for three bottles of the shit. I couldn't help the grin on my face at the image I'd presented Allie with. A drunk as hell bear... She probably thought she was losing her mind.

"Hello? I'm talking to you."

I growled, letting more than a little of my bear poke through. I didn't give a fuck if I scared Eric all the way back to whatever rock he crawled out from under.

"Gentlemen. Allie is feeling better. If you could both keep it down, however, I'm sure that would help. I've got another call. One of you make sure she stays awake. She's got a mild concussion."

I stood as Doctor Mae emerged from the trailer. "Thanks for coming so soon."

She patted me on the shoulder before disappearing into the woods behind the trailer. The woman was strange, but she got the job done.

"I'll keep her up."

I blocked Eric's path and shook my head. "G'won back home. I'm going in now."

I didn't wait for his response. I was desperate to see Allie and to make sure she was okay. I needed to make things right. I was still freaking out about the whole mate thing, but seeing her passed out earlier...it'd scared the hell out of me worse than anything. In the second it took for her body to hit the ground, I'd realized that I couldn't give her up. If I lost her because she didn't want me, and ended up like my mom, then so be it. At least I'd go crazy knowing that I'd fought for us.

She was sitting up on the couch, holding an ice pack to her head. She looked okay, but I could sense that she felt queasy. Her coloring wasn't what it should've been.

When she looked up at me, there was a curiosity in her eyes. "I had a very... errr... interesting dream about you."

I knelt in front of her and smiled. "Oh, yeah? Was I clothed or unclothed?"

Her eyes suddenly lifted and shot to the doorway. "Eric?"

I wanted to spin around and shove the little twerp back out of the door. Fucker couldn't take a hint.

He moved to sit beside her but a warning growl from me had him frozen in his spot. Allie's eyes shot open wide. I ignored her look for the moment, figuring she was piecing together what she'd seen.

"Alyson, let me take you home. I saw your car on the way into town. We'll hire someone to get it back to North Carolina. I'll have all your stuff taken to my house as well. We'll put all this behind us."

Allie frowned. "How did you find me?"

Eric at least had the decency to look embarrassed. "I ran into Georgia. When she didn't ask about you, I figured that she knew where you were. Jimmy leaked that she'd booked a flight to Texas and mentioned that she'd need a car to get down here."

"Jimmy is going to be so fired when Georgia finds out." She shook her head and frowned some more. "That doesn't matter, though. Eric, I told you we were done and I meant it. You cheated on me. So many times."

I watched her face for signs of sorrow, ready to rip Eric's dick off if it looked like she was harboring any lingering pain from the asswipe. Instead, she looked up at me with more confusion and curiosity on her face.

"You forgave me for that."

"No, I ignored it. There's a difference. Just like I ignored the fact that you can be a really controlling jerk. This is over, Eric. I'm sorry I didn't end things sooner. I'm also sorry that you had to come all this way. I'm not leaving with you, though. If I ever decide to leave, it'll be because I'm damn good and ready."

My chest tightened. Did she just say what I think she said? Was my shifter hearing playing tricks on me? "You're staying?"

She adjusted the ice pack and sighed. "I think so. Not because of you, though. You've been a jackass. I'm staying because this place feels like home for some reason. I like Abram and I like my job at the bar. I even like that crazy blonde chick who tried to claw your eyes out the first night we met."

It didn't matter to me right now the reasons why, or that she thought I was a jackass. Hell, I was a jackass, she was right about that. All that mattered was that my mate was staying. I surged forward to embrace her but she put a hand on my chest and stopped me.

"We've got some talking to do first, mister."

Eric did some heavy cursing and then swung around to the door. "Thanks a lot, Allie. Maybe, next time, you'll communicate with someone if you have a problem with what they're doing, instead of just holding it inside."

"Hey, dumbass, women don't like it when you cheat. Duh."

I moved towards the door in case Eric needed help through it. Turns out he didn't. He was out before I reached him, so I flipped the lock before returning to Allie's side. "You okay?"

She was staring up at me and dropped the ice pack into her lap. "It wasn't a dream, was it?"

I sighed. "I'm not sure how much you want to know right now. Maybe we should wait until your brain feels a little better?"

"I'm not sure my brain is ever going to feel okay again."

"Well... here goes, then."

24

ALLIE

"How did... How did you turn into a bear, Thorn?" I half expected him to laugh at me. It was ridiculous, wasn't it? He hadn't actually turned into a bear.

Thorn knelt on an old carpet square in front of me. "That's something I left out of the story about mates."

He leaned back on his heels and looked around. He seemed worried and uncomfortable. He opened his mouth several times, and then closed it again before he'd uttered a single sound as though he wasn't sure where to start.

"Just spill, Thorn."

"I'm a bear shifter. I mean... I can shapeshift into a bear. Bear. Bear shifter." He looked up at the ceiling and groaned. "I turn into a bear. I'm still me, but a bear. A shifter bear."

I didn't know if it was the blow I'd taken to the head or how flustered the big man before me was, but I couldn't help the single laugh that burst from my lips.

His cheeks turned red. "I've never had to explain it before. I don't know how to say it. Jesus, woman. Don't laugh. You're killing me here."

That just turned my single laugh into a fit of giggles. I'd officially lost my mind. The bump must've jumbled things more than the doctor thought.

"Alright," Thorn sighed, "You made me do this."

Before my eyes, fur started sprouting from his body and he opened his mouth to show me his jaw growing and his teeth sharpening. I stopped laughing and slunk farther into my seat.

Then, Thorn shook himself and he was back to normal. "Bear shifter."

"But... that's... just in the movies."

It was his turn to laugh. "It's not. There are all sorts of shifters out there. We just happen to be bears 'round here."

"We?"

"Yeah. A lot of people in this town are shifters. There aren't a lot of other differences between normal humans and us, so it's hard to tell who's who."

I swallowed. "What *are* the differences?"

"You mean besides the shifting into an animal thing? Shifters run hotter. We're always warm to the touch, no matter what. We're usually just a little bigger, too. And...we have mates."

I sat up. "Mates? As in soulmates?"

He nodded. "You're mine."

My chest fluttered. "You think I'm your mate?"

Another nod. "I do."

We were both surprised when my hand shot out and punched him square in the face. He didn't so much as flinch, but I immediately gasped from the pain of my fist contacting his rock-solid jaw. He captured my hand in his and rubbed my knuckles. *Crap.* That was meant to hurt *him* more than it did me.

"Have you known since day one?"

"I knew it. I just... I didn't have a normal upbringing. My mom and stepdad... they weren't exactly the picture of the perfect mating, but that's all I had to go by. Their complete disaster. It scared the hell out of me. It still does. I don't know how to do this. Mating is serious.

I don't know how to be what you deserve, Allie. What if I can't make you happy? If we mate and you decide this isn't for you, it could kill me."

I pulled my hand from his and edged away. My head throbbed but I needed some space. I moved to the other side of the couch and pulled my feet under me. "Literally kill you?"

"It's what happened to my Mom. I told you she went crazy, but it wasn't much longer after her breakdown that she died. Doctor Mae tried to save her, but Mom lost the will to live. Without that, a doctor isn't much good."

"I'm sorry, Thorn. That's horrible." I paused. "Wait... we haven't...*mated,* right?"

He laughed suddenly and the surprising sound filled the trailer. If he noticed the goosebumps it left on my arms and legs, he didn't comment. "No, we definitely haven't mated."

I scooted closer, unable to stop myself. "How do we mate?"

He growled and reached out like he was going to grab me but stopped himself. "Jesus. I'm holding on by a thread here, Allie. I want you. I want this. I've been hiding from you, but that's not working. We're meant to be side by side."

He paused and looked down at his hands, where they rested inches from my legs. "Do you like being called Alyson?"

All my anger and worry was suddenly forgotten. It wasn't gone for good, but in that moment, I wanted just to comfort him. I slid over until I was in front of him and cupped his face. "I prefer Allie. I broke things off with him the night we talked outside, Hawthorne. I realized that I wanted that soulmate thing that you talked about. I don't know why he showed up, but it wasn't because I wanted him here."

"Why aren't you freaking out? Or pissed at me? This doesn't seem normal."

I laughed and then winced from head pain. "To be honest with you, I'm still trying to digest the whole bear thing right now. And I *am* pissed, because you treated me like crap and I deserve better. Especially if I'm your mate."

He growled. "You *are* my mate. No if. Are."

Despite the pain in my head, fireworks were going off in my lower regions. "Can I see it? Can I see your bear again?"

He looked wary. "I don't know, Allie."

I stroked his cheek. "I need to make it real for myself. It still seems too crazy to be real."

"Okay." He stood up and moved away from me. His hands went to his pants and he grinned. "If I don't take them off, they'll end up shredded."

I turned my head and tried to act normally. I heard his pants hit the floor and then the trailer dipped dangerously to one side. I squeaked and then grabbed my head when my own high-pitched sound hurt it.

A loud huffing and a warm gust of air hit me on the back of my neck as the trailer settled again. I looked back, knowing I would see a bear, but still surprised as hell.

He was huge. I'd never seen a bear that close up before. I couldn't help standing up to get a better look. Amazingly, I felt no fear as I reached out and touched his soft fur.

"Do you condition? This feels so good."

Another huff and then the trailer rocked again as he went down on all fours. Even then, he was practically eye level with me. His wet nose nudged me and I laughed.

"Abram didn't give me any rules about animals, but I think he assumed I wouldn't bring a bear into his trailer. You're denting the floor."

He tossed his head back and made a snorting sound that soothed me to my very core. Something about the bear in front of me was as familiar and relaxing as curling up with a warm blanket in front of a cozy fireplace on a cold night. I felt like I'd known the bear forever and that I could trust it with my life. Which, I guess I was doing. Knowing that this was Thorn just added to my warm feelings. He'd felt familiar since the very beginning, too.

I ran my hands over its head and then scratched behind its ears.

In a heartbeat, the bear was Thorn kneeling in front of me, naked as a jaybird, with his head in my hands. I stroked my hand over his hair once more and then moved away.

"You're not freaking out."

I sat on the couch and picked up my ice pack again. "No. Maybe I'll save the freak-out for later. Maybe I won't. I don't know."

His naked ass sat next to me, and damned if he wasn't completely at ease with it. "Does that mean we can be together?"

I turned my head away from him, unwilling to be distracted by all that he had on display. "It means that I'm going to make a serious attempt at processing all of this. You can't expect me to answer tonight, Thorn. You've been hiding from me for days. I don't know if I trust that you won't do it again. You're a bear. The whole town is full of bears. I'm trying to fit into my new 'Allie who won't be walked on by men' persona. My head is being attacked by a sledge hammer. I need time, at least until the headache is gone."

"Okay. I get it. I'm staying here to watch over you, though."

I turned my face to glare at him and I held up my hand to shield his man parts from my view. "No, you can't stay here. I can't think if you're going to be hanging around. I need time to myself."

The pout my words drew from his lips was almost comical. He nodded and stood up, dangling his junk directly in my line of vision. When I slammed my eyes shut, he chuckled. "Sorry. I'll be outside tonight, making sure you don't fall asleep. I'll leave in the morning."

"Just go home, Thorn. I'm really okay. Plus, how do you plan on knowing if I'm asleep from out there?"

He pulled his pants on and smirked. "I can hear your heart beating. Right now, it's racing. If it slows down too much, I'll know that you're falling asleep."

I shook my head and pointed to the door. "One more thing to process."

He was almost out when I thought of something else. "Wait, Thorn. How is mating done, if it's not sex?"

He gripped the door molding and didn't turn back around to face me. "I would... claim you during sex. With a bite. It would leave a mark on you, letting everyone know that you're mine."

I watched him go and leaned back. He had nothing to worry about. With these thoughts buzzing around in my head, there would be no sleep anytime soon.

25

ALLIE

I t'd been a week since I found out about the bear population of Burden. A week of looking at the world through very different eyes. Finding out that people I'd met in Burden, people who in every other aspect appeared to be, well... *people*, were actually bears too. The men, anyway. Even Abram was a shifter. Learning that they weren't what I'd thought wasn't as uncomfortable to me as I might have suspected. To me they were just normal men...who could also become bears.

Seeing was also believing, and Thorn's friends were amazing that week. They each shifted for me and let me see their bears so I knew I wasn't just imagining everything.

I'd also talked to Georgia about it for hours at a time on the phone. It went without saying that the whole shifter thing was something that needed to be kept hush-hush, but I knew Georgia. The woman had never met an idea or challenge that she wasn't willing to face head on. Plus, I'd trust Georgia with my life. I knew she'd take a secret to her grave rather than betray our friendship.

Georgia had been beyond surprised, she was thrilled and excited. In fact, after I'd told her about Thorn, and that I was planning to stay in Burden for a while, maybe indefinitely, she made immediate plans to head to Texas to visit for a little while.

I'd lost all my anger at Thorn the night I found out about shifters, but I'd still kept him at a distance in the beginning of the week. I wanted to see how he was going to react to me when I wasn't being stalked by my ex and recovering from a bump to the head. I didn't really know how this whole mate thing worked. Would he still want me as badly when there wasn't any competition?

I worked at night and explored Burden during the day, doing all I could to get back to feeling normal and to forget about the biting part of mating.

I couldn't deny what I felt for Thorn. The strong connection was there before I even knew about mates. Or shifters. Since then, he'd made so many efforts to get closer to me that our connection had grown stronger.

He was proving that he meant what he said about believing that I was his mate. His eyes stayed on me when he was in the same room as me and when I'd finally give in and look at him, he'd have heat and something softer in his eyes. It was arresting. Seeing such a big man, a man who had power that I didn't even understand, look at me like he would just wither and blow away if I rejected him was heart wrenching. I was his. I was. It was just the biting that I couldn't seem to get past.

He left flowers for me. Granted, they sometimes still had the roots attached, but I gave him credit anyway, because, obviously, the crazy bear wasn't used to giving girls flowers. He also insisted on walking me to and from work every day. I'd turned down all his invitations for dinner at his place, though. It wasn't that I wasn't ready to get on with our relationship. I was just nervous.

Abram had explained to me what a mate was to a shifter and what it meant. Mating with Thorn was a more powerful thing to do than if I went out and married him. Mating was forever. While I didn't doubt my feelings for him, at all, I was terrified of forever. What if he couldn't leave his womanizing ways behind? Without question, I knew if he cheated on me, it wouldn't be like it was with Eric or the others. It would destroy me.

Still, I couldn't stay away from him any longer. I was feeling the absence of his touch. Like an addict, my hands shook when he was near me. It seemed impossible to fight.

But, I had to eventually put on my big girl panties, and tonight was the night. I was giving in— at least to sex with him. I'd made sure to dress in a tiny skirt and a tank top that dipped low. I slipped away from the bar during a lull and carried a beer to his table.

Thorn was sitting in his normal seat, with Hutch, Sam, Sterling, and Wyatt beside him. I smiled at the rest of the guys and then leaned down in front of Thorn. The position gave him an eyeful of cleavage and he didn't miss the chance to look at it.

"I was hoping that maybe you could show me around your place tonight." I put the beer down in front of him and stood back up.

Before I could even turn away, he'd grabbed my arm. He easily picked me up and tossed me over his shoulder. "Abram, cover for us," he shouted across the room.

I felt my face burning as the bar erupted in cheers. "Thorn!"

He slapped my ass hard enough to sting and rushed out of the bar. "Say no and I'll carry you back inside right now, Allie."

I remained silent and held on as he straightened me and put me in the cab of his truck. Instead of rushing around to the driver's side, though, he captured my lips in a kiss, demanding and hot, and I moaned as he slipped his tongue into my mouth and his hands into my hair.

Just as quickly, he was gone. He slammed the door closed and was getting in behind the wheel in a flash. He looked at me with enough heat to light the world on fire, and then started the truck.

I held my breath as he pedal-to-the-metaled it towards his place. I'd planned on at least looking around his place for a few minutes, but his urgency told me that that might have to wait. I felt the same sense of urgency. As soon as he touched me, the need had increased to a nearly painful level. I wanted him. Now.

"You want to be with me forever?" I swore after I asked it. Why had I opened my mouth? Crazy things were bound to come out. I wasn't in control enough to make sure they didn't.

Thorn swung a sharp left and then glanced at me after he straightened the truck. "Yes. I want forever. Do you?"

"You really do?"

He slid to a stop in front of a log cabin style house. "Yes. I really do. That's what I've been trying to show you. I messed up at first. I was too scared to accept what this was. I'm nothing without you, Allie. You're my other half. I would let you go if you wanted me to, but that will never be what I want. I want to claim you and mark you as my own so you know and so every fucker in this town knows that I would die for you. I'm in. I'm in this with everything I have."

I threw myself into his arms, across the console, and wrapped myself around him. It was exactly what I needed to hear. I kissed him with everything I had in me, letting him know how happy he made me.

Thorn pulled me out of the truck, stumbling as I made the job harder by kissing his neck and face. He grabbed my ass and lifted it and held me to him so I could wrap my legs around him. We made it to the door and then fell to the floor in the entryway.

It didn't matter to either of us. Thorn kissed my skin as he exposed it, pulling the tank top down and then ripping it over my head. His hands were everywhere, teasing me.

"I want you to mark me. I want to do this." I said it while gripping his hair and pulling his face up to mine.

Thorn kissed me senseless and yanked my skirt up to my waist. My panties were ripped off and his pants were undone. When he pulled back, his eyes were burning bright. "Forever?"

I tugged at his pants and nodded. "Forever. Do you-?"

He cut me off by rolling us and suddenly brushing the tip of his shaft against my slick folds. He held my gaze as he slowly pushed into me. "Completely."

I wrapped myself around him and buried my face in his neck, feeling entirely overwhelmed with delirious pleasure. This felt different. Knowing he was my mate and that this was going to be forever took it to a whole different intensity than the first time. I could already feel my body tensing for a release.

Thorn thrust himself back and forth inside of me, slow and deep, taking me to levels that I didn't know existed. He braced himself on his elbows on either side of my head, and when I tilted my head back, and our eyes met, I could see that he was just as affected as I was. My world rocked.

"Claim me, Thorn."

He nudged my head to the side and lowered his mouth to my neck. I held my breath as his tongue teased me and licked the sensitive skin. Then he kissed me there. "Relax, Allie. I would never hurt you."

I tilted my hips and he hit an even deeper spot, spurring the first ripples of my orgasm. I cried out and then felt it. Hot pleasure radiated from my neck as I felt his teeth sink in. My orgasm doubled, tripled as I felt Thorn give himself to me completely. A second passed and Thorns body spasmed as he climaxed with me.

Our bodies writhed together until we were both wiped out, exhausting everything in our mating. We were tangled together, our clothes pushed and pulled in ways that made it hard to move, but everything was perfect. I'd never felt so at peace as I did in that moment.

I kept my body wrapped around Thorn's, even as he rolled to his side to hold me. I kept my body wrapped around his, even as I drifted into a blissful sleep.

26

HAWTHORNE

I watched my mate sleeping in my arms, both of us still on the floor. I glanced up at the door, unsure if we'd even closed it. It was pushed most of the way shut, so I ignored it and turned my attentions back to Allie. Her hair was rumpled and a piece clung to her lips as she made a gentle whistling sound. Her body was molded against mine so closely that I couldn't see much but the curve of her waist. Even just that glimpse had me hard again.

Somehow, I hadn't managed to fuck everything up. She still wanted me. After the way I'd been such a jackass to her, I couldn't imagine why. I was grateful, though. She was everything.

After I'd moved past my own fear, it hadn't taken long to realize that she was nothing like my father or my mother. I was nothing like my father or mother. I didn't have to worry about their past becoming my present. I knew Allie, even from just watching her the past week. I was safe with her. And she was safe with me.

Talking to Abram, and some of the other mated guys in town, I'd come to realize that I hadn't understood the mate bond at all. I was fucking lucky I'd found my mate.

She stirred in her sleep and I smiled like an grinnin' fool down at her. Her skirt was still on and the boots she wore hadn't been taken off, either. My pants were still caught around my legs and I'd somehow managed to keep my hat on. I should've felt ashamed for not making the claiming more special for her. But, I couldn't feel anything but happy as a pig in mud that it'd happened. I had a lifetime to make things special. And I'd spend every day of it trying.

Allie stirred again and I pressed my lips to her forehead. When she opened her eyes, they were full of happiness. I grinned back at her. "Hi."

She stretched, exposing the curve of her breast to me. "Hi, yourself."

I rolled us over so she was on top of me and I caught one of her nipples in my mouth. I nipped it gently and then fell back with a groan as she lifted her hips and took me in her hot body again. "Jesus, woman."

She braced herself on my chest and rolled her hips. "Eventually, we should talk more."

I bucked my hips up to meet her. "We'll have plenty of time to talk more once you move in here."

She started to argue but I rolled us over and thrust into her again. "We'll talk later"

With a wicked grin, she raked her nails down my back. "Later, then."

I had a feeling she could talk me into anything. If she didn't want to move in, I'd be staying in the too-small bed of a trailer with newly warped floors. It didn't matter, though. Especially when she licked her lips and rolled us over so she was on top again. I was so lost in euphoria, I had no interest in being found.

Next Book: **Wyatt**

For more books, please visit:

https://books2read.com/candaceayers

https://lovestruckromance.com

Candace Ayers ♡

27192939R00069